# ASHES

### ◆ IONA WAYLAND ◆

First paperback edition October 2020

*Book design by [Damonza]*

*Edited by Stephanie Cohen*

ISBN 978-1-7351588-0-8 (paperback)
ISBN 978-1-7351588-1-5 (ebook)

Published by Twin Trees Press
https://ionawayland.wixsite.com/author

*For all the survivors who braved the forest.*
*And for those still finding their way, trust yourself.*
*Let your intuition guide you.*

*"And into the forest I go, to lose my mind and find my soul."*

—John Muir

*Content warnings include: graphic violence, foul language, homophobic language, sexual situations, abuse, assault, drug usage, and suicide.*

# CHAPTER ONE

THE RIP OF tape is loud in my quiet apartment as I wrap layer after layer to secure the lid on Donny's urn. I place him in the pack along with other survival gear. My brother is cushioned and snug in one of his favorite sweatshirts. It's the soft, blue hoodie he wore on windy days at the beach. It still faintly smells like him, sea salt, and cigarette smoke. I secure Totto, the machete I "had to name so it wouldn't turn on me" to the side. If Donny were here in person, he'd say, "Angela, stop it. Don't go through with this." But, this isn't his decision.

I take my time lacing my hiking boots and folding my socks how the backpacking guy at the trail store showed me. I'm fucking crazy for doing this. I don't know how to hike and can't even remember the last time I worked out. God knows I can barely get myself to leave my apartment. Yet here I am, struggling to lift this giant hiking pack and locking up my apartment for what might be the last time. The place that once radiated warmth, that I called home, is now cold and empty as the key scrapes its way into the lock. But I can't think like that. I need to keep my spirits up – for Donny, for my own survival.

My boots clang against the stairs, slick with morning dew.

The soles of my new boots grip better than I imagined while I make my way down to Donny's beater 1997 Jeep Cherokee that's right where he left it. I don't have a car of my own and it makes me feel like my brother is still with me. I guess by Jessica's standards, his spirit is. I close my eyes and sigh when the engine starts up, bringing a flood of summer memories. We'd just drive, the sun baking our skin. It was easy to laugh then. Donny's smile was always contagious. He'd rest his arm out the window and slap the side of the car to the beat of our music. He'd look at me with his sparkling, dark black eyes that everyone said we shared.

I pull out of the lot a little too fast with a jolting start. I have to get used to the stick shift. Donny's ashes lurch next to me in the passenger's seat of his shitty car while I blare ODESZA and The Chainsmokers. I try to remain open-minded while I drive, just as Jessica advised me. I roll down the window, tasting the brine in the air. The ocean becomes just a thin blue line and then fades out of view. The hours pass and the beach transitions to cornfields, and then forests. As the flat roads undulate, I catch sight of Donny out of the corner of my eye. He faces forward with a dark, sad gaze. When I turn to him, though, my giant backpack is there instead.

The air still feels heavy, like his eyes are on me. I turn off the car's staticky stereo system and take a shaky breath. I want to talk to my brother.

"I know you were probably there when Jessica told me what I needed to do with your essence, and so I have your ashes and everything else on the list. I know I do, because I quadru-ple-checked. It's what's in Hollow Forest that I'm honestly petrified of."

I wait, expecting Donny to respond somehow. Nothing happens.

"She said how important it is to keep calm and not let myself be detected, that the things in there can smell indecisiveness and fear. But why the Hell would she say that? I'm already afraid. Trying not to be makes it even worse." My hands cramp as I grip the steering wheel. "I don't even know what half the words were that she said. Like, what is," I shuffle to grab at the papers with my scrawled writing, my sweaty palms making them damp, "the 'Canid Carey'? She said how it couldn't touch me if I just keep my doubts at bay, like shove them deep down. I do that well already, right?" I give a humorless laugh. "If I just think of it like those haunted hayrides, like I'm doing this on purpose, I've signed up for this – if I don't lose my shit, it, they, whatever, can't hurt me." I force out a sigh.

It's quiet for too long. My face becomes hot and sweat beads at my temples. It's mid-April, but my perspiration has nothing to do with the temperature. With trembling hands, I clutch the steering wheel even tighter, crumpling my notes. It gets difficult to take full breaths, so I turn the electronica back up. It's our music, and I let the pulsing rhythms move through me like a current.

Jessica told me, "Angela, the Hollow feels like an empty heart within the forest itself. It's somewhere in the west, but after that, you need to let your intuition guide you." I felt like she was being so condescending when she said that it was "a calling" and had practically looked down her little nose at me when she told me that if I wasn't *open* enough or *intuitive* enough, that it might not happen at all. Wherever this intuition guides me is where I'll release my brother. I have a little more than a month to figure it out.

Trees flash past until I automatically follow a side road that leads into a wooded area. Dirt and leaves fly back in a cloud behind us. The all-season tires crunch over small rocks and old branches that are strewn across the road, tall trees stretching high above on both sides. It creates a tunnel effect, deep green and shadowed. Bits of golden light reaches into the car and flash between the foliage as we travel.

I'm on the dirt road for about an hour and a half before I feel something. It's a tug at my chest, a flinch in my arm. It's a pull, a compulsion, so clear and instinctive that I drive toward it. I don't even need to use that sage to clear my mind or whatever. It didn't do Donny any good and I'm not going to rely on it, either. A half-mile sails by and I know where to pull off the dirt road.

We are in the right place.

I shove my license, phone, and charger into the console. I'm not meant to bring them.

When I cut the engine, it feels so still. It isn't until I get out and secure my backpack that I realize how completely silent it is. No birds. No pitter-patter of paws on the forest floor. Not even the leaves flutter in the breeze. The zip of nylon straps as I adjust my pack and my unworn boots crunching on pebbles are the only sounds. There is a little incline that gently slopes up from where the road cuts into the earth. I keep my breathing steady as I hike and search. I follow the lure of the pull into the woods. After about a minute of walking, there's a gate, just as Jessica described.

It's worn yet sturdy. With a slightly crooked slant, the short gate tilts between two waist-level posts. The top of Donny's Jeep is still behind me when I look over my shoulder. I can turn back if I want to. But then, who knows where my brother would end up. His soul would be lost forever. I trudge closer to the stand-alone fence. Carved into its rain-stained wood is the message, **KEEP SHUT**.

It's almost comical how I can see over it. If I didn't know

better, I could just walk around or hop over it. But that sign was carved there for a reason. It's there to separate, to keep certain things out, and certain things in. But here I am, willing to walk right into the entrance of Hollow Forest. The air is thick and hazy. My hair stands on end as I draw closer. My throat tightens when I unlatch the gate. Tears prick my eyes and I fight the tingling in my legs that beg me to run away while the pull feels like it's singing in my skull. He was gone. I didn't have to do this. If I walked in, I might never walk out. Why would I risk myself? But my brother was someone, is someone, I'd die for. I picture Donny, before it all. He's telling one of his corny jokes. I can almost hear his raspy laughter. He deserved to laugh again. A sob rakes its way through my chest, but I swallow it down.

The chain is heavier than I thought it would be and feels cold and scratchy from the rust buildup. It scrapes and clunks as my quivering hands untangle the slackening links. I open the gate just enough for me to slip through. The same warning is carved on the inside. I take care to latch it again before turning around to face what's ahead. I can't see the Jeep or the road anymore; it's like I'm suddenly in the thick of the forest. I force myself to take a deep breath through my silent tears and trek toward the magnetic pull.

5

# CHAPTER TWO

It's no longer silent. Everything vibrates with noise, teems with life. It smells overwhelmingly of pine and sap so sweet, I taste it in the air. I stop for a moment to gaze at a tree that has bark as smooth as polished leather. I let my hands lightly brush against the trunks, but stop when there's scurrying beneath it. Donny clangs against my back as I trudge deeper.

I don't know if I can tell you when my brother Donny actually left me. It could have been when my parents kicked him out. Possibly, it was when he first stole pills or when he transitioned to piercing his veins with poison. Or maybe, it was when his beloved Zach was gone. I just know that he's been restless for as long as I remember, even before his death.

Donny was seven and a half years older than me, and he always said that it was his job to protect his "Angelita". He and I had different views on what protection really was, though. Donny thought that meant he should keep the fact that he liked boys a secret. The look of relief on his face when I said "I already know" after he finally came out made my heart crack in two.

Everyone danced around his desires like he was contaminated. My parents thought I didn't know why he was kicked out when he turned eighteen. They tried to say they didn't like his "lifestyle," and that now that he was an adult, he had to leave if he was going to "act that way." Which is laughable, because it just forced him to move in with his first boyfriend anyway. But I should have stood up for him. I should have told my parents that their conditional love started chipping away at him long ago. I was part of the problem, a part of Donny's hurt.

Maybe that's why he always felt like he was in pain. Once, when he visited me in my college dorm, he just popped a pill right in front of me. When I looked at him, horrified, he realized that he hadn't hidden his habit. It was such an easy motion for him. No thought, just a tilt of his head, a gulp, and he was off to oblivion. Donny tried to say they were antibiotics. Antibiotics? Come on. And I continued to play along, forever accepting my role as the innocent angel everyone thought I was.

At first, I thought the pills were a phase, an experimentation. But soon I began to worry. He'd throw some back after we grabbed dinner before he'd get in the car with me, and sometimes he'd chase some pills with beer he smuggled into my dorm. What could I do, though? Confront him and drive him away? What if he stopped visiting me? I had already missed him for huge parts of my life because my parents wouldn't let him attend with whatever guy he was dating at the time. My high school graduation, taking pictures before prom, when I got my license – he wasn't there. He'd meet me afterward and treat me to dinner and I'd show him pictures, but it wasn't the same. But now, he was consistently in my life and I didn't want to mess that up. We talked freely and had adventures without the angsty sighs, silent tears, and a heavy dose of disappointed head-shaking. If he had my support, then maybe it could undo the damage he was dealt from my family.

So I included him in everything. I told him about my classes in mass communication, the podcast I was working on that delved into myths and legends, and introduced him to my friends. We'd talk about the guys we liked and I took him to some college parties. But it only got worse when he entered the party scene. He melted into my university's raves like he belonged there. He was an eel in a sea of strobe lights and MDMA. After a crazy night, he'd crash at my dorm on a blow-up mattress. We'd talk all night about his adventures and then he'd sleep all day. My roomie thought he was hot with his dark, sad eyes, so she didn't complain. That homme fatale look really hooked her.

Donny would use thick eyeliner and take careful precision with his curls as if he wasn't going to be completely covered in sweat later and mess up his artwork anyway. He'd spend hours picking out my outfit and helping me with my cat-eye that I never could make symmetrical. Then we would go out. He searched with ferocity for something that would make him whole. Something or someone that could complete him enough so that he could drown out the guilt and disappointment my parents had layered over him, causing him to suffocate. I used to go with him until I got swallowed whole. It's funny, really. All that talk of machismo and wanting to protect, and yet my brother left me at those parties to fend for myself. I had to claw my way back to reality to try and make my life normal again.

It was when I was ditched at one of those raves that he found Zach. He and my dad are so much alike. They just don't know it, or don't want to acknowledge it. Donny is attracted to naiveté, like my dad always had been. That's why my dad chose my mom when she was new to America with her Latina views of *el flechazo* and without knowing a word of English. He wanted to wrap someone in comfort and wisdom. He wanted someone that looked up to him with stars in their eyes. That had to have been what Donny saw in Zach. That newly-out, music majoring, oboe-playing, freshman spirit zapped Donny like a lightning rod.

The first time I met Zach, Don was high and glassy-eyed with his guyliner smudged and his laughter rasping from inhaling nothing but smoke the entire night. Zach nervously greeted me, with those big, blue eyes. Zach looked like he was plucked straight out of the Midwest with his sandy hair, khakis, and billions of freckles speckling his skin. He was freshly combed and had chapped lips from kissing his very first guy. Zach probably felt like his world would be so much better. I felt sick, knowing I probably looked like that, too. Knowing that was probably why I had been hunted and gobbled up when I went to those parties. Why I was hand-picked by *him*. I try not to think about all the things I could have done differently. I'm fixing it now.

The trees are denser as I walk. Even with the special gel packs, my shoulders are sore. My feet are killing me worst of all and I have to sit down for a minute to check them out.

When I unlace my boots, it feels like I'm opening a dam. The looser it gets, the more pain my feet are in. There are stains on the bottom of my socks and the balls of my feet sting. I peel off one of my socks and it rolls up in a sweaty bunch of cloth. Blood drips down my upraised foot and slowly makes its way down my ankle. Somehow, seeing the fresh blood makes it hurt even more. I wince when I take off my other sock. Huffing, I drag my backpack over to me and dig around Donny's urn for the little First Aid kit. I put some antibiotic ointment on my open blisters, and pry the lid off of the Band-Aid tin.

"Ooo, that looks like a nasty wound there."

I jump and practically dump all the Band-Aids from the tin. It's a woman's voice that comes from deeper in the woods. I look for the source of the voice. A young woman makes her way toward me. She has a long, messy, dirty-blonde braid that hangs over her shoulder. She must be about thirty and a fellow backpacker. She's carrying a decked-out pack. There's a tent roll that Jessica told me not to bring secured at the top of her supplies. I think of how adamant Jessica was when she said: *Always sleep within view of the sky.* No tent for me, just a bare sleeping bag. The woman also has one of those water pouches that has a straw leading from the backpack right to her shoulder so she can take a drink whenever she needs to be refreshed. Her skin has a golden glow to it, and her eyes sparkle.

"Are you alright? That looks like it hurts a lot," she says, her voice like honey.

"Yeah. I'm fine. It just serves me right for not breaking in my hiking boots before going out on this venture." I want to laugh in relief.

"Been there," she says. She takes off her humongous backpack and gently sits it on the ground across from me.

A chill runs down my spine when she squats down to look at my foot and tilts her head when she sees the blood trail. I use a cotton ball to wipe it away. This lady is a bit too focused on it.

"I'm fine. I swear," I say, slapping some Band-Aids on the bottom of my feet. I can wrap it later. I'm too vulnerable barefoot.

"Have you backpacked for very long?" she asks, standing up while I lace my boots back up. My feet protest the entire time.

"Nope, this is my first time." I try to cram the kit back into my bag. She cranes her neck to see what's inside.

"What's that?" she asks, pointing at the little glint of Donny's silver-brushed urn peeping through the sweatshirt. Her forehead creases with concern.

"Just some extra clothes," I say, zipping up the bag. I'm not asking her what's in her bag. Though, maybe she's here for similar reasons as me. Maybe she's just looking for a comrade, or maybe she's laid someone to rest, too. "How long have you been backpacking?" I ask.

"Oh, it feels like forever." She smiles but looks tired. Crow's feet crease the outside corners of her eyes.

"Well, you definitely know what you're doing, it looks like." I motion at her pack on the ground. When I look at her backpack, it appears more weathered and has some holes in it that I hadn't noticed before. I greedily try to catch a glimpse of anything through the holes inside her pack. She picks it up, though, and secures it on her back and around her waist.

"Yeah. I made sure to get the best of the best." Her braid is knocked a little looser and is fraying. "I didn't know how long I'd be out here." There's a hint of melancholy to her voice.

"How long did it take you?" I ask, dancing around the elephant in the room. "You must be close to the end because you're going back to the gate."

Her eyes are wide. "You know where the gate is? Can you show me?"

She grips my shoulders, and when I look at her hands, they look thin and not as golden as before. I gasp. It's as if her face has aged a decade in just a second.

"Y-yes. Um, it's back that way." I jerk a thumb over my shoulder, showing the way I came from. "It's about a two-hour hike."

"You don't understand, do you?" Tears stream down her wrinkled cheeks. "There are no directions here, only intuition. I don't have it."

She releases my shoulders to cry into her hands. I stare at the top of her head as she sobs and shakes. Her hair has dulled and her backpack is missing the tent. There's a slash in the side where her water pouch had been. She and her pack are covered in mud splotches, dirt, and pieces of dead leaves and grass.

"But, you have to. How did you find the gate in the first place?" The pull is so clear. I just know where to go.

"I didn't find it," she screeches, probably exhausted from crying and carrying and searching. She looks up at me, her face taut and wrinkled, her hair thin and missing in patches, her cheeks sunken in. Her voice wavers and is difficult for her to control. "I followed someone in here. I wanted to help them. My friend," she says, spitting out some of her teeth when she said the word 'friend'.

I cringe as her yellowed teeth fall on the leaves at my feet, making a pitter-patter like rain would.

"You just have t-to, you have to," I stammer as her bones protrude, her thin skin stretching over them, "be open. You have to open your mind and let yourself feel—"

But she won't be feeling anything anymore. She's a corpse and then dust, just like my brother.

With numb hands, I hoist my pack on my back. I have to get away from here. Electric pulses run through my limbs. Despite Jessica's warnings to remain calm and steady, I sprint as fast as I can, flight taking hold. Each footfall and leap stings, but it makes me feel like I'm real and still alive. Panting and sweating, I allow Hollow Forest to suck me in deeper, grateful for the lure, grateful I'm not lost.

# CHAPTER THREE

Nighttime descends. The further I follow my instincts, the thicker the forest becomes. It isn't until I trip over a branch and fall, the sticks and brambles piercing my hands, that I decide to bed down for the night. I try to shake off my fear of seeing that woman wither away in front of me by continuing forward, but her shrunken face and rattling bones pop into my mind, making me itchy. I dig at my arms and neck, not knowing if it's from skittering insects or if I'm checking that I'm still flesh and bone. I don't want to stop progressing. I want to put as much space between me and that woman as I can, but it would be foolish and reckless of me to continue exhausted and stumbling around in the dark.

I unroll a sleeping mat, patting it down as flat as I can. I take out my sleeping bag and its waterproof fabric glides over the mat. Jessica had grabbed my wrist when she told me how important it was that I don't fall asleep with something blocking my view of the sky. So no tents, not too many blankets, not even an eye mask. It doesn't make sense with so many trees clustered together. It's constantly shaded and leaves blot out the sky, anyway. She hadn't known why, but she thought perhaps it was important that the universe connect with me when I'm vulnerable or something. She told me she'd try and send me "mind messages" and it would only be possible in the open, if she even could at all. She had that same meltdown when I asked about flashlights or starting a fire. I couldn't produce any light or communication. That apparently was a no-go because it would mess with forces I couldn't begin to understand. So here I am, outside, stuck in the middle of the woods with half-known rules of the forest, and my brother strapped to my back.

I create the boundary Jessica showed me. All I do is draw a large diamond in the soft forest floor with a stick. The boundary acts as a protectant around where I'll sleep. After making myself as packed as possible on the uneven ground, I slip into my sleeping bag. Even with the added sleeping pad under me, it's much harder than my pillow-top memory foam mattress. I feel like I've been spun tight in a spider's web, waiting to be eaten. I try to focus on how tightly I'm zipped in and that people pay good money to wrap themselves in anxiety blankets like this, instead of how much I'm shivering with fear. I don't know if Jessica is right, but for now, she needs to be.

I still remember how ridiculously inseparable Donny and Zach were. A tight laugh escapes my lips when I recall how my brother had just up and left for his new boyfriend and how ironic it is that here he is, literally stuck with me when it had been like pulling teeth to get him to spend any kind of normal amount of time with me once he got with Zach.

When Zach and Donny first started dating, they both spent most of their time at my dorm. When my roomie found out Donny was gay, she got annoyed pretty quickly with their sleepovers. So Donny learned that he couldn't spend as much time at my place anymore.

I didn't realize how much I wanted him to plead and beg to stay until he and Zach moved off-campus without a second thought. I told myself that I needed space from them anyway, that my brother needed this. It was progress. He deserved true love. But it didn't dull the familiar ache of missing out on a brother I always needed.

While Zach and my brother started their new life, I was busy graduating early, adding my own spin to my cozy one-bedroom apartment, and finding a job that wouldn't make me leave all too often. I found the perfect job almost immediately. It somewhat utilized my Mass Communications degree and I telecommuted to assist customers with their complaints and questions. It was all done from my headset, a company laptop, and the comfort of my kitchen table. The apartment I found was newly built, and my landlord was kind and kept to herself. I found such solace in having my own place. It wasn't very big, and that made me feel safe like the walls were hugging and welcoming me. I painted with soft blues and light greens. I got a new comforter, decorative pillows, and a just-like-new floral couch. When I found a print of Georgia O'Keeffe's "Lake George's Reflection" and hung it on the wall, I felt at peace. I had finally found *home*.

Ever since my graduation from the university scene, Donny and Zach became entirely enmeshed. I called Donny a couple times a week only to realize later that I was actually on speakerphone the entire time. I'd find that I was speaking to both of them when Zach would pipe up with advice like "Just look on the bright side," or "You just need to apply yourself." Sometimes they'd invite me over to their place and I'd look forward to talking something out with Donny or need his listening ear. I'd try to hang out with them both, but mid-conversation Donny would get distracted by Zach's dimples and just want to touch him. So the conversation would fade away to Zach's perfect giggles after Donny had started a tickle fight. I should have said something then along the lines of "grow the fuck up". But Zach never would grow the fuck up. Donny killed his innocence before he ever had a chance. I wince at the thought and close my eyes from the past. I try and find a place that's neither here nor there in my mind and listen to the world around me. The hum of the woods is dull and constant. Occasionally, there are scurries in the night or scratches on tree bark close by. Some things crawl and slither past just outside of the diamond. It sounds small and light, so I try to take comfort in the fact that it isn't that withered woman again or the Canid Carey, whatever that was. I guess the smell of my doubts hadn't drawn the largest predator in Hollow Forest my way. Maybe it's because I feel protected in my boundary, or maybe it's because, in one day, it was more exercise than I've had in the past four years combined. No matter the reason, I drift off to sleep. It isn't a sound sleep or without nightmares, but it's something.

# CHAPTER FOUR

I WAKE UP to the sound of scuffling close to me. I open my eyes and blink away a thin stream of light that fought its way through the branches and leaves to touch my face. I must have made the barrier too narrow because part of my pack had been kicked outside the diamond during the night.

Rummaging around my pack is a skinny, almost-naked kid. His entire upper body is within my backpack, desperately digging around and trying to drag it outside the boundary. I grab the bottom end of it and pull, hard. He isn't expecting it and is forced partially into the barrier, screaming. The smell of burnt flesh and hair hit me as he leaps and tumbles backward. I scream too.

He looks like an emaciated little boy with cloth underwear – that is, until I see his head. It's a white goat's head, with little nubbed horns protruding, his tongue sticking out and ears flopping while he screams and stares at his arm. It's been singed by the boundary. I try to drag my bag the rest of the way in, but I pull too quickly and the contents spill and roll. I hug my mostly empty bag to my chest and watch in horror as my food supply and Donny tumble farther from my reach.

He turns, tilting his head to get a good look with his yellow, slitted eyes. He screams again, but this time it's directed at me. He drops to his hands and knees and grabs at the items. He goes right for the food. His ribs rise and fall as he pants. Each spinal bone protrudes as he hunches to grab at the rations. I stumble to my feet, my socks slipping on my silky sleeping bag and I almost fall out of the barrier.

But when he reaches out to get my granola bar, his rectangular pupils dilate as the wrapper falls apart and the granola bar itself crumbled into rich, dark soil in his palms, teeming with insects and worms. The goat boy goes to the next bit of food and watches with what looks like delight as each food item turns to soil. Mounds of rich earth form wherever he touches. It isn't until he turned his gaze on Donny that I scramble to my feet.

He awkwardly crawls on all fours toward Donny's urn. I rip through my pack, holding my breath until I find the machete at the bottom. I slide it from the vinyl covering and step out of the boundary, my fists shaking. The goat boy grabs Donny, swaddled in his sweatshirt, and begins to jump up and down as the fibers fray and eventually became threads in his grasp. It's when his little hands meet the silver urn that his jaw falls open in what looks like surprise.

He hungers for what's inside. He digs at the sweatshirt, revealing the lid of the urn, and tears at the duct tape. It doesn't take him long for the tape to turn to dirt in his grip. My fear and surprise is replaced with rage when he's that close to desecrating my brother. I'm ready.

When he rips at the lid, I run at him. I raise my machete, Totto, high into the air. He turns at the noises and drops my brother. The urn *thunks* to the ground and some of Donny's ashes spill out. The goat boy runs at me, his head down. He head-butts me in the gut, knocking the wind out of me. I fall on my ass with him on top of me and the machete flies just out of reach.

I scurry to get up, but the boy, with more strength than I expect from such a skinny kid, puts his hands on my shoulders and tries to hold me down. My thick sweatshirt withers and little holes form as if moths had chewed them. I get one leg up and I flip on my side, sending him tumbling. I grab Totto again and stumble toward him, but trip. I let my weight bring the machete down on him. It slices easily into his arm. He and I both shriek.

Our faces are so close that our noses almost touch. His mouth foams and frothy spit gets caught in his wispy beard as he scoots away from me. His breath smells like decay and overturned earth. I stand up to slice at him again, but he's too quick. He gets up and runs, clutching his arm tightly to his chest and leaving dark, earthen footprints behind where his bare feet pound against the forest floor.

I snatch up Donny's urn and try to scoop as much of his ashes back in. I practically fall into the diamond again, panting. Sobs choke out as I rock back and forth, clinging to my brother. I originally thought that the only thing at stake was my life, but what if Donny's essence got into the wrong hands? Would he be lost forever? I've only been in Hollow Forest for one night and I've barely survived. I rest my head on Donny, but cry out again when the sweatshirt no longer smells like him. Instead, it reeks of that goat boy's putrid patchouli scent.

That's when I can't shove away those doubtful thoughts as they enter my mind. Jessica told me this would happen, but that I just shouldn't act on them, or I'd leave a trail for the Canid Carey to follow. If she was even right. She certainly hadn't warned me about the goat boy. And what the Hell was that woman who crumbled in front of me? Did Jessica even know *anything*? I sit there, in the diamond, wondering how long I can just wait there and not have to leave. Wondering if there was anything I was told that I could trust.

I stay and watch as what little morning light that could filter through the trees get brighter and brighter. It's much later than I plan on beginning my trek. My muscles are sore and tight, like boulders and pebbles are under my skin instead of muscles. My back and neck are stiff from laying on the ground. I don't know if I can bear to stand up, let alone move forward.

But the pull to move is stronger than ever. It pulses, rushing my veins with purpose, making my heart sing with passion. My chest thrusts forward and my eyes twitch. I hone in on the pull to tell me that what I'm doing is right, that it will be what saves my brother's soul. I can't control the fact that the goat boy destroyed all my food, but what I can control is securing my brother's urn. With each strip of tape, I breathe a little easier. I wrap him in his sweatshirt, taking my time to carefully place it upright in my backpack. I take off my old socks and bandage my blistered feet.

I know I need my boots. They're strewn in the brush, outside of my protected space, out where the monsters are. I stand up, take a breath, and I sprint out of the diamond to retrieve my boots. Pins and needles shoot through my heels as blood rushes down to my blistered feet. I spring back into the boundary. I gingerly put my feet in each boot and lace them up, tight. I salvage what items I can. The goat boy has significantly reduced my food supply and dumped my water everywhere.

The world spins when I turn to face the direction of the pull, my beacon. I focus on my booted feet on the ground and let Hollow Forest hold me up. I pretend I have roots that are so deep that I can't fall over. I can't break. I take a deep breath, remembering Jessica's warnings not to run or doubt or check over my shoulder. It's like I'm breathing the color fern green. There's new life, wet earth, and cool air. I make the sign of the cross, face the direction of my intuition, and move forward.

# CHAPTER FIVE

THEY SAY IT's an epidemic, and that is the most understated thing I've heard in my life. Somehow, "epidemic" doesn't seem to touch on what an alluring and abusive relationship opioids are. I don't know when Donny made the shift from pill-popping to shooting up. My guess is that the fortitude it takes to get yourself to shove a needle in your arm isn't so difficult when your altered brain tells your body that heroin is necessary to live.

Zach tried to be the wall between my brother and his drugs. He, like me, foolishly thought that if he just loved deeply enough, then Donny's need to numb himself would stop. Instead of love conquering all, Zach couldn't fight my brother's demons and succumbed to his influence.

He hadn't even started Zach on pills. Donny led him straight into the miserable nest of needles he created for himself. Sometimes I wonder if Zach got to feel his first high before his lungs became too heavy and tired to breathe, or if he just gave way to eternal sleep on that hot July night.

The dealer went to jail. Zach's body went back to Utah. My parents remained distant and sanctimonious. And after his hospital stay, Donny came to live with me.

Watching my brother spiral was the most difficult thing I've ever experienced, but I knew how he'd be on his own. There was this glimmer of hope that when Donny moved in, that he'd feel secure and supported. I made the mistake of thinking that physical closeness meant safety. In reality, it just meant I had a front-row seat to his self-destruction.

I shake my head, trying to clear my thoughts. The constant tramp and stomp of my heavy feet is hypnotizing. My surroundings appear the same. The trunks and rocks I pass look like I'm walking in an endless loop, yet the pull lets me know I'm progressing the way I'm supposed to. I spend hours trying to pace myself. My tongue is dry and sticks to the roof of my mouth. My fluids are wicking away into sweat. How long can a person go without water? Three days? Two? Pangs of hunger shoot through me and I'm dizzy. I clench my hands into fists so they don't shake as much. My stomach growls in protest to my day of hiking and lack of food.

But my incessant worries are halted when I hear something. It starts as a high, piercing whistle and ends in a rumble that dips so deeply, my ears pop. The forest is still, worried. No creature makes a sound. I keep my pace, feeling like an intruder and watched while I walk as lightly as I can.

That howl has to be the Canid Carey. Jessica warned me of its call and told me not to look back. She said I would start checking and not be able to stop, and that it would only increase my fear and doubt. It takes everything I have to continue through the thick foliage at a steady pace. My heart pounds like a muted drum that shakes my rib cage. My limbs quake, ready to propel me forward in an instant. I know what to do to protect myself from the Canid Carey. I have to stay calm. If I follow the rules, it can't touch me. But I'm at war with my panic.

What if Jessica is wrong?

I play the mind tricks that help me remain calm. I look at each tree, so dense, the sky looks like shards of glass above. Each leaf is so unique in shape and feel. Some crinkly, some waxy. Yet all similar in their green spectrum. They range from yellowish to a dark, hunter hue. Heavenly shimmers of light that fight through the canopy touch the forest floor. It almost gives me hope. Until I smell it.

Its wet fur makes my nose curl. Its footsteps, soft. I shiver, despite the heavy humidity. *Just don't look at it. Don't acknowledge it, even as it whispers your name.*

"Angela. Annngelaaaa."

Like a sigh.

The ground that had just been soil and moss patches grows thick and unruly. Thorny bushes that were far and few between become dense and only let me walk in a few steps at a time before I have to hack at them with my machete. I slice through the brambles that seem to be coming closer and cocooning me. Thorns catch on my arms and legs, easily piercing through the thick fabric. They drag in long, shallow scratches that sting with my sweat.

The Canid smells my fear and doubt. I keep a steady pace while I take off my backpack and swing it around so I have it on the front of my body. I clutch it. The urn is solid through the nylon fabric. He used to give the best hugs. My brother can't hug me back, but I sure as Hell can hold on to him.

I slash at more brambles. They unfurl and grab at me. The oily smell of the stalking beast is overpowering. When Jessica closed her eyes and tried to explain the Canid, she turned white and said that if I followed the rules, I never would have to see the monstrosity. I don't want to know what I'm up against.

The brambles are taller the more I cut into them. They stretch and curl upward to make a dense barrier. I'm barely making headway. A branch scrapes at my scalp, making me gasp. I reach up and tug, ripping several strands loose. I put my hand on my head, smoothing down my hair. I think I see a clearing through the intertwining bramble wall. I move closer and use the repetitive slicing to focus my mind rather than allow the fear to paralyze me.

More branches rake my scalp again, clutching chunks of hair and snapping my head back. Trickles of blood run down my face where they claw my forehead. I struggle to move. I'm so close to the clearing, but my hair is ensnared. My breathing labors and hitches. I can't turn or move my head.

Tears prick my eyes as memories of that terrible night in college flood my mind. I brace myself, fighting the intrusive thoughts and scenes from when I met him at that party. I push aside the phantom feeling of his hands grabbing and yanking my hair.

I have to cut myself out.

Before I can hack, the machete twists grotesquely in my sweaty grip. The blade is aimed at me. It has its own force, its own strength. There's an eagerness that wants to slice my exposed throat. My arm shakes as I battle it back. It slips in my slick palms, just a bit closer, inches from ending me. It strokes my cheek, just like he used to, making it sting as it cut a thin line down the side of my face.

The Canid pants. It's so close to me, just through the thicket.

"Stop," I yell. Air wells inside me and I can't breathe out. Black spots my vision. "I'm not afraid of you."

The machete jumps to my throat and presses ever so gently, calling my bluff. My arms quiver as I fight it back. The brambles constrict and yank my hair back, baring my neck. My entire body shakes, but I can't let the Canid win.

The machete is finished playing with its prey. It swings out dramatically to gain momentum. I try and lock my elbow, but it plunges toward my throat.

"Totto, no!" I shriek.

It stops millimeters from my neck.

*You have to name your knife, or it will turn on you.* I had finally said the ward out loud.

I struggle to put my arm down. Totto is stuck midair, unsure.

"Totto," I say, my voice wavering, "don't attack me again."

I try to lean back, away from its sharp tip that's still pointed at me. Thorns cut into my back, making me gasp. I'm held so tightly, I can't even turn my head.

I gulp and know I need to cut my hair. "Totto, cut me loose."

No movement.

"Totto," I swallow again, the blade somehow feeling confused in my hands, "cut me loose. Cut my," I sob, "cut my hair."

I cry out as Totto yanks, ripping my scalp from the briars and trying to tow me out. But my hair still tethers me. Totto flies high in the air, as high as my arm can reach, and comes down, slicing off my tangled clumps of hair. My arm goes slack, and I drop the machete. I fall to my knees in relief. My neck is cold and goose-bumps rise as black, jagged strands brush my shoulders, cheeks, and nape of my neck. Totto lays on the ground innocently. Just an inanimate object. But I know better.

"Totto, we need to get to the clearing." I clutch the machete with the last of my strength.

We chop and hack through the rest of the thicket with a new fierceness. The brambles rustle and part to allow us through. I stumble into the little clearing, unable to sense the Canid anymore. No more dampened footfalls or excited breaths. The creature disappeared as quickly as it arrived. I center myself with the Hollow's ambiance. It's returned to its busy, bustling ways. Leaves are fluttering. Winged creatures chirping to each other, and what is that? Tears of relief come to my eyes.

Water.

I sprint toward that beautiful sound of a current rushing over stones. My pack clangs against me as I bolt.

I practically run into the creek, sliding through the mud on my knees when I reach the embankment. My backpack plops to the ground and I pull out my pouch, refilling it with clear, cold water. I splash some on my face. The salt left behind from my sweat is gritty on my cheeks and forehead. I wash away some of the blood that's already begun to dry. I cup some to my lips with shaking hands and the water slides down my throat with a chill.

Right before Donny died, we sat on the beach together. We rolled up our jeans, the cold sand under us, and let the freezing waves foam at our toes until they were numb. We hadn't had to say anything. We just looked at the stars over the undulating, black water. Even though we were beach people, I know Donny would have loved this river.

My aching muscles relax, and the more at ease I become, the more exhausted I am. My joints are gum bands, barely holding me together. My feet pulse in pain. I throw off my boots, socks, and bandages. I sink my feet into the cold water. A moan escapes my lips. I can't leave this place.

# CHAPTER SIX

THERE WERE WEEKS when Donny cried himself to sleep on the couch. The first night he stayed with me, his curly hair was matted on one side and his tears drenched the cushions. A damp spot remained for the entire next day. If I hadn't propped it up in the window, it would've stayed wet forever. My parents called a lot, saying they didn't understand why I was letting my "sick and confused" brother stay with me. How could I convey to them that a light inside him flickered out when he poisoned his love, that he lost the perfect person he was trying to mold, or that his diseased mind was hungry for more? Always just a little bit more. How could I show them that he was also getting better? That if they loved and supported him like me, that there were bright spots within the chaos. That he grocery shopped sometimes or wrote inspirational quotes and left them on my laptop before I started the workday. They would never understand it. They would only dismiss and deny, as always. That's what they were good at.

Every morning I'd go to the little kitchen table and do my quality assurance. There was no end to bitchy customer calls and scammers. I would keep a calm voice. Yes, the company was oh so sorry. Yes, we could definitely help them with their "mishap" or "mistake". Yes, I was happy to file their complaint. I worked ten- to twelve-hour shifts every day in my cozy kitchen with a cup of hot tea.

When I took breaks, I would peek into the living room. Donny sat on the same spot on the couch, staring at nothing. On days when he had a little more energy, he'd lay curled up and scrolling through pictures of himself and Zach. One time I battled my issues with confrontation, looked him in his sad, dark eyes, and suggested that he talk to someone. He gave a weak laugh at that.

"Then what, Angela? It won't bring him back. It doesn't change the fact that I killed him."

"You didn't kill him." I tried to soothe my brother and knelt down to eye level. But my words were empty. We both knew that Zach would still be running around campus, maybe competing for first-chair oboe in a symphony orchestra, maybe being the vice president of Pride Club, if he hadn't met my brother.

"I did. And he was so much better than me, Angelita. He was so good, like you." He covered his face with his hands.

My stomach churned. "He loved you, you know."

"I know." Donny choked on the words. "If only I could switch places with him."

"Donny, are you thinking about—" The words caught in my throat.

"No. I'm not going to off myself, Angela. I just miss him like crazy, and if anyone deserves to have OD'd," he put a hand on his chest, "it's me."

Hot anger made me jerk upright. It didn't have to be a him-or-me situation. No one had to OD. But in Donny's world, he thought it was an inevitable way to go. Not an if, but a when.

"Don't be mad, Angelita. I don't mean it. I just wish I could talk to him. I wish I could tell him sorry, and that I love him. If there even is anything after this fucked-up lifetime."

I stood there and stared down at my crumpled brother. He always seemed so big to me. All my memories of Donny were of him towering over everyone. He wasn't quite five-foot-eight, but he had a memorable presence. He was louder, more outgoing, older. But now he had shrunk to half that size. He was withdrawn and weak. He was a flower that had been plucked and was slowly wilting without his roots.

"Just one more time, Angela. That's all I'd need. Just for him to know that I miss him and love him and that I'm so Goddamn disgusted with myself for what I let happen to him. What I led him into."

And that's when the hideous seed was planted. It was the beginning of Donny's demise.

I snap myself out of my memories by setting up my safe area, this time making the diamond a little bigger, and clipping the backpack onto the sleeping bag itself. I change into different clothes, shedding my sweat-soaked, worn layers for new ones. My stomach rumbles angrily and I clutch it. I don't remember a time in my life when I was hungrier. With a watering mouth, I torture myself with images of my mom and Abuelita's special *aji de gallina* and its creamy sauce that warms me up. Or even some *arroz con sopa* could quench my thirst a little and replenish the salt I lost.

While bedding down in the fading light, I tell myself I could live with the hunger. I mean, I'm a bit pudgy. It's not like I'm going to starve to death or anything. But nausea boils in my stomach, my sugar levels dipping too low, and a headache forms from lack of food. If only I was a nature gal who could identify edible plants, nuts, and fruits. Other than little family trips to local farms when I was much younger, I've never hunted and gathered in my life. But my eyes land on a bush next to the river that I hadn't noticed before.

It's a raspberry bush. And not just one. There were tons of them on the other side of the stream behind a clump of trees. I sensed they were there. Of all the things that could be staring me in the face, this was a deliberate answer to my prayers. Maybe this stream was a base for travelers, like a safe zone? I'd needed water, and after my close call with the Canid, here it was. Maybe the Hollow could sense my empty, pitted stomach and provide me with what it could.

With hurried steps, I go to the edge of the creek. There are uneven stones that peep up above the water and lead to the other side. I carefully leap to each slick rock. My bare feet spread and balance. The water is deep, but I can see the river rocks through the slight current. The clarity gives me courage.

I make it across and go straight for the berries. They are tart, yet sweet. Juice runs out of my mouth and down my chin as I gobble them up. They are plentiful. It's relieving that I can stock up on them tomorrow before I carry on.

Once I have my fill, I start back to cross the river. Each step is a bit slicker, a bit wobbly. It was easier to cross the first time. The darkness is settling and makes it more difficult. I jump to the next rock and have to pinwheel my arms to stay upright. Then the next rock. This one is a bit wider and flatter. I slip and almost do a split. I gasp as I strain to bring my legs back together.

Drool leaks out of my mouth. I try to wipe it away and my lip is numb. I wipe my chin and almost smack myself in the face. My hand is limp. I slip forward. I'm three-quarters of the way across. I just have to make it back to the boundary.

I jump to the next rock and my legs buckle. My knee scrapes

on the rock and icy water engulfs me. The stream is like a freezing spear. My chest is tight as I gasp for air. The water would be at waist level if I could hold myself upright, but I'm slumping. The current is stronger than I thought. But that can't be right. My limbs are tingly and numb. My shoulders jerk back, trying to keep me above water while my arms swim to the bank. I kick off the rocky river bottom, my toes pushing against the stones to propel me.

I reach the bank and have to crawl toward the boundary. My arm gives out and my face hits the dirt. My jaw is slack and stuck open, soil sticking in my mouth. I push the dirt out with my tongue. Only my left arm is somewhat working and I use that to scoot forward while kicking my legs. Every inch is excruciating. My mind races while stuck in a useless body. I'm a foot from the boundary when I go completely slack. Something grabs my shoulder and flips me on my back. My hairs stand on end. My eyes go wide, not believing it to be true.

It's him.

# CHAPTER SEVEN

NOT AGAIN. NOT again. Not again. Not again.

"There you are, Angela. I've been looking all over for you."

His disarmingly beautiful, hideous, charming, predatory smile spreads across his face.

It can't be him. It's impossible.

"Jacob, what are you doing here?" I try to ask, but all that comes out are chokes and gurgles. My tongue is thick with beer like the last time I saw him. Back when I was a stupid teenager trying to impress him at that rave. Back when my selfish brother left me at that party.

"Shh, just relax." He puts his arm under my neck, cradling me with a gentleness that I know he isn't capable of. He's too vulturine for that. He's toying with me.

I try to squirm out of his embrace, but my head just lolls to the side. I try to scream, but my breathing is shallow and I barely inhale. I only wheeze as tears stream down my face.

"Aw, don't cry." He wipes away my tears. "Don't you love me? I'm just helping you relax."

He leans down and kisses me. My mouth is invaded by his tongue. I want to spit in his face. I only drool more. He lays me a different way so I'm more prone on the forest floor. He kneels next to me, turning my head so I have to face him. Layer by layer he unwraps me. The cold air from the nearby stream blows against my bare skin. Goosebumps cover my naked body. He takes off his shirt. His waistband barely rests on his narrow hips. He climbs on top of me. Hips pressing hard against mine. I squeeze my eyes shut, making more tears spill. I focus on the leaves under my back. I reach my hand out to feel for a weapon, but my fingers only twitch.

The movement draws his attention and he grabs my hands, lacing his fingers through mine. His erection is hard against me. I suck in air, trying to make any noise at all. To tell him it isn't okay. That I'm not trash. That I graduated. That I have my own apartment. That I've managed to have a day or two where I don't picture him. That I've grown so much since freshman year. That I can't be dragged back into that pit of anguish he dug out in my mind. That I don't think I can live if I have to go through this again.

He sucks on my neck, my breasts, works his way down, and licks at my inner thighs. Sometimes, his arms brush me with feathers, but when my eyes dart to the sensation, it's just his skin. When I focus on his hideous face, his evil face, his lying face, his hunting face, his nose grows hooked and pointed and his eyes big and wide, as large as saucers. What the fuck did he give me?

He takes off his pants and kneels over my head, his penis inches from my mouth. One hand is massaging my scalp, making it tingle. He wraps my jaggedly cut hair around his fist and yanks.

He leans in close, those cool eyes that had lured me in. The same eyes I looked into while we danced and the strobe lights reflected. The same eyes that became excited when we walked on the beach. The same eyes all the girls in my dorm gushed over.

The eyes that had twinkled when I gulped down the laced drink. The eyes I had nightmares about. The eyes that flashed in the depths of my mind when I finally feel free.

"Don't bite me." The threat is clear. He doesn't have to say what he'd do. He wouldn't hesitate to tell everyone I wanted it. I was disposable. I was his plaything.

He shoves his penis into my mouth, but it turns to freezing cold liquid and washes down my throat. That's when I fight.

I scream. I thrash. My arms swing wildly in fists, finally free from their immobile state. I curse at Jacob with every word I know. I make some up. I kick at his balls. I bite at his penis that is no longer there. I go to shove him off my chest, the pressure making it difficult to breathe.

My head and shoulders are resting on the marshy river bank. Water soaks into my clothes that are somehow still on my body. A feathered beast of some sort is crushing me with its dead weight. I try to make out what it is. It's like a dumpy woman covered in white feathers. Her greasy hair flops in my face while her giant, owl-like eyes stare, unblinking at me. She's dead. Black, inky blood runs out of her and warms my chest and stomach while my hair and neck freeze in the water.

I shove it off me and someone grabs for my shoulders. I scratch at them; a fine white mist rises from where my bloody claw marks should be. The arms draw back for a second and then splash water on my face. I bite the hand, my teeth sinking all the way through the skin between the pointer finger and thumb. Mist rolls out of where my bite should be, like dry ice, and then condenses back together to make a whole hand. The arms yank back.

I roll over on all fours. I vomit into the river. Again. Then again. Then again. The stream washes away my pink, sweet sick.

"Good. Get that shit out of your system," says a voice.

I jump to my feet with fists clenched, and my teeth bared.

Across from me is a man wearing a skull on his head. The skull has a longish snout and eight-point antlers that sweep up and reach toward the leafy canopy. He's wrapped in some kind of leather skirt, as if he took a shower and wrapped a towel around himself. The man grabs the end of the skull by sticking his fingers in the nasal cavities and lifts it up so it sits back on his head. It reveals a freckled face with round, sable eyes, wide with concern. Long, thick dreads hang around his shoulders. Blood spatters his dark, brown skin. His chest and arms are flecked with the same inky blood that spilled from the creature. He holds up his hands, bloodied palms facing me.

"Owletta got you good, huh?" He nods at the feathered carcass I'd thrown off me.

"What?"

He sees me staring at the feathered heap. "Yeah. That's Owletta. She feeds off of your worst fear. Depending on how much of those poisonous berries you eat, she makes the nightmare more vivid."

My limbs still shake with adrenaline.

"I thought you were a Stain at first, but when I saw Owletta just crouched over you, I tried to drag you away to splash some water on your face, but she was too attached.""

"Jesus, everything is attached to me."

"They're all starving. They're hunting for life. They thrive on it."

"Well, I'm still fucking alive! They've got a Goddamn *feast* right here."

"Hush your voice." He takes a tentative step toward me. "I had to kill her, but the Canid can smell my blood. Come on. You need a safe place. Follow me."

I laugh. It's one step away from becoming sobs.

"Safe? I'm not going anywhere with you."

I bolt to where all my stuff is and dive into the diamond barrier, busting my lip against Donny's urn. I hug him tight, wishing he was here. My blood-soaked clothes squelch as I hold him tighter.

"Hey, please, come with me." He says in a soft voice and kneels down on one knee, reaching a hand out for me to take.

"Get away from me," I hiss. I'm a feral thing trying to survive in a world I don't understand.

"Please." His voice is soothing. He inches closer, making his antlers sway.

"Go!" I growl. I can't trust a voice like his, a kindness like his.

"I know you're scared. I was too, at first. I can show you the ropes. I know where we can be completely protected."

It's too good to be true. He's probably tricking me.

As if he reads my mind, he says, "I'm not one of the Fiends that live here."

"Why did you turn to mist, then?" I spit.

"I can explain, but we need to go. I'm settled not too far from here."

I stay as still as stone.

"Look, if I were one of those, could I reach through this Fiend screen?" He knows I'm confused and says, "This diamond. Has anything tried to get through, and couldn't?"

Yes. It worked before. The goat boy was burned by it. I nod.

"Then you know how it works. It sears them, but just until they get past the line. The Canid Carey could smash right through. The barrier's too weak, and you've been traumatized. It'll smell your vulnerability in a second. I'm begging you, follow me. I wouldn't be able to reach my hand in without getting scorched if I was a Fiend."

Everything in me screams not to trust him, to curl up in a ball, to cry, to never move again. Standing up in that moment is one of the most difficult things I've ever done. I take his hand, warming my frozen one, and steady myself. He tries to pack my bag for me before I smack his hands away, not wanting him near my brother.

He holds his hands up. "Sorry, this is your shit. I'm gonna grab the Owletta. She's a good kill, and we can make you blend in more. I'll give you some space," he says. His eyes are wide and darting. He's trying to remain calm, but I know I should hurry.

I pack up my stuff with quivering, numb hands and secure my backpack. I make my way to the guy who already has the big owl-woman creature flung over his shoulder as if it's an old towel. It was so heavy to me.

"Follow me," he says, pulling the deer skull back down over his face. "We are close, but we have to move quickly."

And I follow him. His antlers rattle and lead me astray into Hollow Forest.

# CHAPTER EIGHT

THE WALK STARTS silently. Our footsteps are muffled by the pine needles and moss that carpet the ground. The Owletta's ugly beaked head bobs and lolls with each stride. Her orbic eyes stare at nothing and her thin skin is pulled taut where the hooked beak attaches to her face. I try to focus on something else other than her dead, hideous visage. The sway of the reaching antlers and the stranger's locks are mesmerizing as he guides me deeper into Hollow Forest. A rolling mist rises in front of us and only reveals a few thick, tall trees at a time. Some of them have triangular, diamond, and cross-like etchings carved into their flaking trunks where the bark is peeled.

I promised myself that I would never trust someone so soothing, so disarming. It meant they had a history of luring people, and I didn't want to be the victim again. If Donny were here, actually here, then he'd be able to tell me whether this guy could be trusted. I knew once I walked through that gate, that we wouldn't be able to communicate anymore. Not like we had been. I'd give anything to speak with him again. Just like Donny would have given anything to speak to Zach again. Just one last time.

That "one last time" idea was where the interest began. And

by interest, I really mean obsession. Donny had been without energy for so long that he had to start small. He would lay in the fetal position on the couch with his phone. But instead of passively staring at selfies, he was researching. Christianity, Mormonism, Daoism, Hinduism, Judaism, Islamism, Wicca. What did each of those have to offer? An afterlife that Donny couldn't wait to sink his faith and hope into. He had to, or it meant that Zach was gone for good.

He started experimenting with attending mosques and temples. I liked that he included me in a few adventures. We could soak up the culture while he explained what he learned. Though he had to fight off a panic attack beforehand, he even attended a church service. He entered a yoga and meditation club. It wasn't until he met with a guy who said he could find Donny's spirit guide that it got out of control. Donny would flip tarot cards before he'd even leave my apartment. I'd cough and sputter when he burned sage and put crystals in circular formations. The smell was so overpowering that sometimes I had to crack a window. It was that book, though, that made my skin crawl.

"What's that?" I asked when he first brought it home.

He clutched it so tightly. It was a hardback with a plain, blue cover. It looked like a worn novel that lost its jacket.

Don's eyes lit up and he gave that wide smile he always did when he thought he had a grand plan. I knew it well. It happened when he had a bad idea.

"A book," he said.

*Yeah no shit*, I thought. I sighed. "What kind of book?"

"This book will help me be able to talk to Zach again. I just need to talk to him one more time, Angela. Just tell him I love him." His voice got hoarse. "And beg him to forgive me."

I gave him a weak smile before putting my headset back on.

The sickly, overpowering smell of sage burned my nostrils, and it was difficult to concentrate on calls. They say that shit is supposed to be relaxing. No way. It made me choke up, to the point where one of the customers on the other line asked if I was okay. But I'd be Goddamned if I was going to interrupt something that might give my brother peace. He would just need to rip through this new phase, and then maybe move onto something else.

When I finished my calls, it was late, later than usual. I had been trying to give him space and privacy, which was difficult in my tiny apartment. It was a win-win, though. The more calls I completed, the better chance of a bonus, which meant my resentment of Donny not paying for rent or food might subside.

By the time I took the headset off, my ears were sore. The scripted phone conversation had buzzed so loudly in my mind, that at first, I hadn't noticed Don chuckling to himself. I had thought that he was just watching TV with headphones in or something, because it had been all day since he had started his ritual attempt. I mean, how long could you chant or pray or whatever?

But there he was, sage smoking, some candles melting, and Donny, talking to a fucking book like a lunatic.

"Donny?" I hesitated.

Something stopped me from walking over to him. It felt like there was a bubble of pressure between the kitchen and the living room.

Don whipped around and glared at me, confused. "What?" he snapped and gave his head a little shake.

He must have seen me take a step back because he said, "Sorry, I was in the middle of it."

"Did it work?" I asked.

"Oh, yeah!" His face lit up.

I felt queasy at the sight of his big smile.

"Oh my gosh, Ange, I've found him! He told me he's okay and that he forgives me." He gave a short, quick laugh. "Can you believe that, Ange? He forgives me. He always was such a big-hearted guy like that. He wouldn't hold a grudge. He always saw the good in people. He brought the best out in me, you know?"

"Yeah." But I didn't. I just saw Zach as someone whose naiveté enabled Donny. "So you talked to—"

"Yes! This is the first time I've felt relief. I finally feel free, you know? And I didn't realize how much I had missed him. And don't have that look on your face. I'm *supposed* to be able to talk to him. It's part of the whole thing. It means it's working."

"Can you see him?" I tried not to let the fear creep into my voice.

"No, no. He said he's not a person anymore. He's a spirit, and we can't see things like that, Ange."

Oh right, how could I ask a stupid question like that? I suppressed an eye roll at his cocky tone.

"So you can hear him? Like, in your ears?"

"Yeah, it sounds like he's sitting right here with me – at least, until *you* walked over."

"Well, it's not like it's very large in here. I mean, I tried to keep my distance, but I'm going to wind down before bed."

Don sneered. "Okay, Abuela." He saw my confused look and said, "Early night tonight? Did you need to take a half-day or something?"

"It's almost nine. I worked overtime," I said, trying not to let my voice catch in my surprise.

"What?" He was airy, his gaze distant. There was a lightness and ease to his smile.

"Look at your phone," was all I could say.

"Holy shit! I must have been so wrapped up in talking to Zach. It was so great to hear his voice again, you know?"

"Yeah, I bet it was. I'm glad you were able to find closure."

And I honestly was.

Maybe this was a way for him to move on from his rock-bottom and be more himself. We'd have more moments of Soloman sibling time. We'd make fun of scary movies together and he'd burn the popcorn. He'd bug me to get makeup with him. He already had been bugging me to get out of the apartment more often. Those glimpses of my real brother were getting more frequent and lasting much longer. He finally had what he needed. This was the last little bit that could help him heal.

"Closure is such a great word for it. Yeah, I got some closure. And I can't wait to talk to him again tomorrow."

"What?"

"Well, I didn't get to tell him everything, and it'll be the anniversary of his death in three and a half months. I need to tell him about the memorial I had for him, and how all of his bandmates showed up. And how that one girl who had a crush on him and didn't know he was gay sang his favorite song."

"You're going to tell him about his own memorial?" My stomach churned.

"Yeah! He said he didn't have a connection with anyone after he died because no one tried hard enough, and that I'm the only one that went looking for him. Can you believe that? His own parents didn't even try all the things I tried."

Leave it to fucking Donny to be a protector to Zach, even in the afterlife.

"I thought that you wanted to say your apologies, say your goodbyes, and—"

"And what?" Don's tone stabbed at me.

I was silent.

"And what, Ange? Never talk to him again?"

Well yeah, because Donny was alive and Zach was dead, and that's typically how things go. Not to mention that he sat there and talked to the guy for like, twelve hours already.

"I love you, and you're a great sister, so don't be mad. But you just don't get it. I've been trying to work on myself, get past this, and I've literally found a way to speak to someone about it. You're always telling me to talk to someone."

Yeah. A living, breathing therapist.

"And now I finally have! And I had to dig deep for this book. It wasn't cheap, either."

Where did he get the money, when he couldn't pay for rent or food? Maybe he was selling my stuff again. There was that pain, that emptiness that happened when my glimmers of hope for his recovery were crushed. Why did I let myself get excited? I should have known.

"And you want me to give it up after just a one-time use?"

I wanted to argue what he said, but his eyes told me that it was non-negotiable. I just sighed, went to the bathroom, brushed my teeth, and got into bed. Don followed my lead soon after, and he stopped in the doorway of my bedroom while I watched *Modern Family* on my phone. It wasn't to say goodnight.

"It doesn't work right now."

"What doesn't work?"

"The words in the book. I can't hear Zach."

"Well, maybe it ran out of energy, like batteries?" I didn't want to hear Zach's name again.

"Um, I don't think that's how it works. He just stopped

talking when you walked in the room. I think I have to really concentrate. Maybe I'm the one who doesn't have energy."

"Yeah maybe that, too." He was seriously losing it.

"I'll try again tomorrow, but maybe, you know, your headset is portable so . . ."

I looked at him.

"So maybe you could take it, maybe you could, like . . . ."

I wanted to test if he was ungrateful enough to finish that thought. I wasn't going to offer. I wasn't going to give him any more of myself. I kept my lips closed and my gaze steady.

"Maybe you could do your work at the library or something."

My hands shook. I was trying not to get so mad at him, but I wanted to scream. Instead, I said, "You're trying to kick me out of my own apartment?"

He shook his head, instantly regretting his words. "No, no you're right. And Zach was always shy. But he knows you. Heck, he even told me that he wasn't comfortable talking to me anywhere other than your place. It's probably not you, and I know how much you hate leaving, you little hermit."

He gave me that I'm-sorry-I-was-just-an-asshole smile that didn't work on me and went back to the living room to try and sleep on the couch. Maybe he needed to talk to Zach one more time to clear things up. Or maybe I was too desperate for my brother to fix himself that I didn't see how sick he had become.

A stick snaps under my stride. The man and I jump at the sudden sound.

He glances over his shoulder and asks "What's your name?" in a voice just above a whisper.

"Angela Soloman." I'm hoarse. "What's yours?"

"Bond. James Bond," he says with a hearty chuckle and stops for a second. He turns to face me.

I raise my eyebrows.

"What? You don't like double-oh-seven? The best of the best? He's honestly my hero, and I pretend I'm on a mission sometimes so that I can do what I need to do." His words are coming out too fast. He's too excited. "I can never get the theme song out of my head. It just replays and replays." There's a smile in his voice even though his face was shielded by the skull mask. "Really? You don't like Bond?"

"I never said that," I say, uneasy.

"For real though, it's Wyatt. Just Wyatt."

"Okay, just Wyatt. Why are we stopping?"

"We're here. See, through the fog?" He points slightly to the right.

There are shadows or outlines of something. It's kind of like a lumpy dome. It reminds me of a giant turtle shell, silhouetted in the mist. "Yeah?"

"Well, that's where we are about to go."

I take a step toward it.

"Hold up, hold up. Wait a second," Wyatt says.

He walks up to a tree with triangular markings and knocks three times. He goes to the one next to it with the same markings and knocks three more times. There's scurrying and scratching beneath the bark that makes my skin crawl. It's like the blue hardcover book's clawing and knocking.

"What are you doing?" I ask.

"Have you ever heard 'knock three times' for good luck? Or 'knock on wood?'"

"Yeah, of course."

"Well, there's something to that," he says.

The mist thins and he walks to two more trees that have diamonds carved into a smooth place where the bark was removed. Sticky, golden sap drizzles down the etchings. He knocks on both of them. We stroll to the left where the next two are unveiled by the fog. These have intersecting circles carved into their birch-like trunks.

We repeat that pattern. Find two trees, knock three times, and so on. We follow this invisible trail marked by tree symbols until we find twin evergreens that have crosses etched in them. When I see the crosses, the tension eases in my shoulders. This is what I'm familiar with. This is what I used to grow in faith, how I found hope.

# CHAPTER NINE

THE GROUND IS flat and moss-covered in the clearing. The trees form a nearly perfect circle around the large camp. My feet rest on wet earth. There are little diamonds everywhere etched into the ground. They intersect and radiate out around the circumference of the tree line. There's a *hiss* and *pop* as we cross over them and some of the Owletta's feathers become blackened and singed.

A loud snort makes me jump. There's a large, hairless horse in front of us. It has mottled pink-and-gray skin and a dark gray mane and tail. It stands close to the entrance and seems to look at us, even though its eyes are a milky white, its pupils glazed with film. Its ears are faced forward, alert, and a wide hoof paws at the ground. A jagged, leather strap around its neck secures it to a tree.

"Don't worry. That's Laken," Wyatt says, petting it on its grayish muzzle.

"What the fuck is it?"

"I call her a seahorse, because she can swim really well. She tried to drown me the first time I encountered her."

"So you kept her?"

"She was just scared of me at first, and I totally understand the feeling," he says, gazing into her filmy eyes. "But I wanted to show you this." He waves his arm at his abode.

My eyes hadn't tricked me. Up ahead, there's a large dome made of interwoven branches and twigs packed together with mud and moss. It's like a giant bird's nest flipped upside down. A cave of branches. Wyatt dumps the Owletta with a sigh and leads me to the dome. He pushes a leather pelt in the doorway aside to reveal a cozy, darkened space within.

There's a stump that has what looks like a half-eaten meal of raw meat resting on it. A rock has various knives and spears delicately aligned in a row. To the side is a bed of moss and leaves that's indented.

"*Mi casa es su casa*," he says, taking off his mask. "It's been a while since I've had guests here."

That's a bit creepy, but I'm thankful to be around another person. Even if it's a scam and I'm going to die, I'd rather die with a little hospitality.

"Thanks for letting me stay," I whisper.

"You don't have to whisper. We lost it," he says. "It doesn't hunt by sound or smell like we think. The Canid Carey is drawn to despair, doubt, and pain."

He reminds me of the know-it-all kid in my freshman philosophy class.

He gives a nervous laugh. "And it only really comes this far into Hollow Forest boundaries when it gets a whiff of me. But we're safe in here."

"Oh, good." I grip my pack's straps and wish my big brother was here with me. He was always a good backup.

"Listen, the diamonds you were drawing won't work so well, but you got the idea."

He's so overeager to tell me all the shit I did wrong.

"The mist gets thicker when I 'knocked on wood' to make a whole one-way mirror effect. And you know those electric dog fences? Well that's what all those symbols make when interlaced, except more than a thousand of them. I made sure of that. We basically have an invisible barrier." He puts his hands on his hips, proud to tell someone about his work.

"No Fiends can get in. Not even that big baddy. Not unless they know where to knock." He raps his knuckles on his forehead before giving it a little shake. "Don't worry about that, though. Let's focus on this great catch here. I have one more friend for you to meet."

A wide, triumphant smile spreads across his face. As if I wasn't already terrified. As if I knew what he meant by "friend." He leads me back outside to the clearing.

Wyatt cups his hands to his mouth and gives a trilled call. Soundlessly, a rusty red colored bird with at least a seven-foot wingspan circles above us. Each spiral brings the gigantic creature closer. Wyatt gives a sharp whistle, and the bird dives straight toward us. I cry out when it's about to spear me. Instead, it whips up and gracefully lands on a branch close to Wyatt's shoulder. It carefully folds its wings back and cocks its head to the side. It has wild, white-blue eyes with pinpoint pupils and a black beak with a little beard under it.

"What is that?" I take a few steps back.

"This is Skeletor," he says, brimming with pride.

"Skeletor?"

"I know, not very original. Laken came from a lake, and Skeletor here, well, he likes to eat bones. He's, like, a vulture of some kind, I think."

I shiver.

"So, all we have to do is throw Owletta into the air a bit, and our good buddy Skeletor will do the rest. Check this out."

He rushes over to the carcass like a kid who couldn't wait one second more before opening their presents. He grabs its taloned feet and drags it further into the mossy clearing. Skeletor bobs his head, excited for what's about to happen. The Owletta has more of a woman's body. There are hips and a hag-like face that comes to a point at the sharp beak. White feathers cover its body except for the top of its head. White, stringy hair falls from the crown of its scalp. Its hair drags behind it as Wyatt pulls. Several white feathers detach and leave a sparse trail.

"Grab the Owletta's wings, closer to her torso. Yeah, there." His breath is quick, excited. "Help me hoist her into the air."

I hesitantly grab her wings. At the end are grayish, scaly fingers tipped with talon-like nails.

"On the count of three, we are going to swing her into the air."

"One." We lift her off the ground.

"Two." We give a test swing like we're two trees and she's a hammock. Skeletor spreads his wings.

"Three," he yells.

We release her and the lumpy, feathered body flies through the air. Skeletor flaps wildly and rushes at it. His feet grip it, and hoist it higher and higher. It's heavy for him, but he manages to take the Fiend clear to the top of the trees, above the canopy. He releases. The Owletta's lifeless body plummets and lands with a crack. The joints angle in impossible directions and it's split right open. Skeletor dives at her and tears at her body.

I puke. Again.

"Oh no. I'm so sorry. I thought this would comfort you."

Concern laces his voice. "It almost consumed you. I thought you'd want to, like, get it back."

He doesn't know what would make me feel better. He'd just assumed, like everyone else.

"This doesn't make me feel better," I say. My tongue is too thick for my mouth.

"I'm sorry. I'm really sorry. This is the kind of stuff that makes me feel better. That's all."

"Mutilating things makes you feel better?"

We both look over at Skeletor, who's trying and struggling to swallow a femur bone whole.

"No, like, it took advantage of you when you were seeing what you were seeing."

I don't want to think about it. "What the fuck do you know?"

Wyatt's eyes grow wide. "Look, I'm really sorry. Tell me what you saw, maybe I can—"

"What. Help? I don't even know what the fuck you are. You're like, a mist person or something. And you have a God-damn naked horse and a vulture thing that eats bones and has a stupid-ass name."

"That bad, huh? You must have eaten a lot of berries. I did too, the first time. Luckily The Rot was the only thing that found me when I was like that, and they're pretty shy."

"What words are even coming out of your mouth?"

"I'm sorry. The Rot is like a kid body with a goat head."

"That goat thing? The walking compost bin?"

"Yeah. I'm not trying to scare you. I'm trying to be here for you. I get stuck in and out of here and I believe that my goal is to help other people out. I've been here for I don't even know how long. There's so much I do to make sense of this Hell, and it's probably really shocking to you. How long have you been here?" He can't stop the corners of his mouth from flickering upward.

"Two nights."

"Wow. Okay. You're a real newbie."

I want to punch him.

"So you probably came in through a gate, right?"

"Yeah. I did. I drove until I felt that pull."

"Gotcha. Well, I'm not really here the same way you are. Sometimes I just show up, and sometimes I disappear, especially when I'm injured."

"Into mist?"

"Exactly. And things don't seem to hurt me, but if they make enough parts of my body into mist, then I'll disappear for a while before I come back."

"Where?" I ask.

"I'm not really sure. I'm not even sure I'm alive anymore, to be honest with you. But I still have the pull, here. It's usually with travelers through these parts. That's why I knew to help you. I felt a pull by the river." He smiles.

"Thanks," I mumble, trying to block out what I just went through, trying to ignore the ripping, tearing, and crunching of bones that Skeletor makes.

I'm so tired. Tired of walking. Tired of being afraid. I shouldn't believe it so easily, but this place seems safe. Maybe it's the number of diamonds everywhere. I hadn't thought to interlace them like a chain-link fence, and Jessica said that the smaller they are, the better, and I guess there's no limit to how many I can make.

As if reading my mind again, Wyatt says, "You must be exhausted, and honestly, you've been really lucky to have made it this deep into the forest and not become a Stain."

I give him a confused look. My face feels tight from where my brows have been furrowed.

"It's okay. We can talk about it another time, but it's late. You can take the moss bed," he says, making his way to the dome.

He digs around in a pack that sits next to the stump. "Here." He hands me a tanned hide. It has brown fur on one side. "Sometimes there's a chill at night. You can use this to keep you warm."

It smells putrid. "No. Thank you, though. I have a sleeping bag."

He's hurt. "Right. Good idea. I'll use the hide as my bed and I'll sleep out by Laken, so don't worry. I won't bother you while you rest, and I'll try not to startle you."

"Thanks," I say to his retreating back. I unroll my sleeping bag on the moss and dried leaves.

Can I even sleep? After being assaulted by Jacob again, being vulnerable in front of a strange man, seeing new Hollow Forest creatures, and knowing that Jessica was wrong about a couple of things, I'm wired. I wasn't given full instruction on the diamonds. Jessica hadn't told me what the Canid actually is. She left out so much. What else didn't I know about? But my lids are somehow heavy and my mind is numb. I eventually fall into a disturbed sleep filled with restlessness, Jessica's distant words, and images of Donny's book.

# CHAPTER TEN

THE WORN BOOK became exceedingly present in our lives. The spine was cracked, and any time Donny wanted to talk to Zach, it would open right to the page he needed. He'd sit in the middle of the living room cross-legged, let the book fall open, say a few words, and then look like he was watching a TV in his lap. Luckily, my headset drowned out his talking and laughter.

He always waited until I started my work for the day. He'd say his good mornings, whistle a little tune, and start setting up with pep in his step. It wasn't the listless plodding that I was used to. He woke every day with a new purpose. I put on my headset, listened to complaints and cursing from the caller, and then my line crackled. It was a zapping click like someone was listening to my call.

Having someone monitoring calls isn't all that unusual. Sometimes people do it just to make sure quality assurance has quality. Retail and customer satisfaction are like a black hole. It became so commonplace that I grew to expect the zap and click on the line after the putrid sage crept into my sinuses.

It wasn't until one of my monthly reviews with my boss, Mr. Cleary, that I learned he had only listened to one call and gave me an "outstanding service" review. The next time there was a click, I put the customer on hold and carefully removed my headset. Donny talked and laughed like usual. I was nosy and tried to eavesdrop. I smiled when the one-sided conversation I overheard sounded as boring as ever.

Sometimes, I believed or at least wanted to believe, that Donny just wanted Zach back so badly, he was making up what he would say to him. Like that empty chair thing I did once in therapy. And I thought, *it's fine*. He didn't have bruised inner-elbows. Hidden needles hadn't rolled out from under the couch. Keep burning that motherfucking sage and do your séance if you have to. More power to you. I tried to ignore my growing fear that maybe there was something to this book. Would it have a power so large that it would cause interference with my call?

But I was lying to myself as much as Donny was lying to himself. When I took off that headset to listen, Donny might laugh or talk or something, but then he'd stop mid-sentence and sit in silence. One time, I made an excuse to walk into the living room, and Don just stared at me when I entered. I gave him a little wave, and he didn't respond.

I asked him, "How's it going in here," and just, nothing. No response. Not a blink.

I was so uncomfortable that I narrated my own movements out loud to him. "Here I go, walking to check and see if we got mail." And his eyes followed me as I walked to the door, and again when I came back and sat back down at the kitchen table to work. And it wasn't until I put the headphones back on and started to work, that I heard the click. He was talking to Zach again.

Should I have had Donny committed? He wasn't harming himself, but he was still sick. He didn't feel like my brother. A chill gripped my gut as I finished my calls.

After about a week and a half of his unhealthy behavior, I had reached a point where I was over it. Donny would thank me a bunch for letting him stay in the apartment. He'd tell me what great progress he was making in his healing process. Blah blah blah. He must have felt my growing distaste for him talking to the dead in my living room because he was really trying to work me over. But I played and replayed what I'd say to him.

"Donny, maybe you need a break?" I said it like a coward to the back of his head while he was making us scrambled eggs one morning.

It was basically the only thing he knew how to cook, but I loved it when he did it. When he was getting clean, the smell of scrambled eggs filling the apartment was a sign he was himself again. I hoped I wasn't making a mistake.

My hands began to shake when I saw his back stiffen. He didn't say anything, so I tried again. "Maybe, we could go on a walk today, like we always liked to do. It's only March, so the boardwalk won't be busy with drunk spring breakers yet." I tried to make my voice light and unwavering.

He turned around slowly, pan sizzling on the stove, and he smiled at me. But it wasn't his dimpled smile, his toothy smile, or his up-to-no-good smile. It was even and curled on one side, never reaching his eyes.

"That's funny," he said in a smooth tone.

"What do you mean?" I said.

"That you're even thinking about leaving the apartment. I didn't think you could. But like you said, those partiers won't be there. You wouldn't want to be around drunk teenagers, now would you?"

"What the fuck, Don?"

"Don't want any bad memories popping up," he said coolly.

My voice hitched in my throat and tears burned at the corner of my eyes. He just froze like that, a bit too still, with that stupid-ass grin on his face, until the eggs started to burn. He whipped around and lifted the pan off the stove.

"Shit! I burnt the damn eggs. Angela, why do I always mess stuff up?" He laughed with his familiar laugh and turned, searching desperately for a plate to pile the eggs onto.

"I don't know, Don."

I stalked off to my room. I didn't care that he burnt them. I didn't have an appetite anyway.

# CHAPTER ELEVEN

THE SLIDE AND clink of knives wakes me. I sit up and my uneven hair brushes against my face. I peek past the flap that covers the dome's opening. Wyatt sharpens two black knives against each other over and over again. They scrape and grate like gnashing, metal teeth.

Laken lays on the ground. Her massive body sits on her folded legs while her milky eyes stare at nothing. Her ears rotate and twitch to Wyatt's work. Skeletor perches on a low branch, his head tilted.

The Owletta carcass is completely flat, devoid of bones and organs. Only a blood-stained, feathered body is left. Her disgusting skull is missing and I try not to gag. I open the hide flap a little more and Laken's scream rings through the air. I shudder.

"Well, look who slept in," he says smiling, not missing a beat with his sharpening.

"What time is it?"

"Hell if I know. I don't think there is such a thing as time here. Only nights. There are always nights."

This guy's so fucking weird.

"What are you doing?" I ask, even though I'm sure I don't want to know.

"I'm making something for you so that we can go hunting," he said. "It's almost finished."

I hesitantly walk over to him. He picks up the Owletta hide and I wince when he rakes at the little pieces of flesh still stuck to the thin membrane of skin. Donny's flat, dead eyes flash into my mind and my throat tightens.

"You don't have to watch, you know." An edginess creeps into his voice.

"I know, I just, I just wanted to see what you were doing."

"Well, if you give me a second, I'll put some salt and clay on this hide, and you can wear it. It'll keep you sort of hidden. Like, the Fiends will think you're just another one of them most of the time. As long as you're confident when you wear it, you'll blend right in. They're hungry shits, but most of them aren't smart. I was only found out one time. Though it might be because I have the skull of a Ruminant. No one wants to mess with one of those, except crazies like me. Its pelt and skull were too good to ignore."

He carefully lays the hide flat on the ground, spreading it out evenly with the feather side down. The thin membrane has barely any fat or meat left on it. Wyatt layers a pile of the chunky salt and dried clay powder over it in thick strokes. Oils from the skin make his dark skin shine and the salt sticks between his fingers. He stands back to admire his work and allows Laken to lick the salt from his hands. I put the back of my hand to my mouth so that he won't see how grossed out I am. Skeletor spreads his wings, but Wyatt hisses and spits in response. The vulture tucks them back in, understanding the message. This was Wyatt's now.

He turns to me, smiling. His eyes dart from me to the hide and back to me, waiting for praise.

"This is very nice. Thank you," I say, trying to focus on anything else other than these three tameless creatures in front of me. "It must have taken a long time."

"It used to," he says proudly, "but after years of doing this, I've got it down. This'll be ready by the time we get back from going for a little scavenging mission."

"Oh, we're going scavenging?"

He doesn't answer me while he hums the James Bond theme song, collecting his gear. There's something off with how he's walking. It's too tense. I shouldn't go on a stroll through the dangerous woods with a stranger anyway, let alone when he's moving like that. I've survived enough to know that you don't let that kind of shit go.

"What's the deal?" I say, crossing my arms tightly over my chest.

His lips get tight. "I accidentally did something I didn't mean to."

Well, he's not a bullshitter. That's for sure. I grow hot.

"I went to get Charm and City."

"Who?"

"These." He twirls his black knives to demonstrate. "You've gotta name them."

"I know," I say, annoyed with the eagerness I feel to reassure him that I'm aware of at least some of the rules. Even though Jessica turned out to be wrong about the Canid and how to draw the diamonds.

"Good! Well, I named them after where I was born."

"Baltimore?"

"Yep. Are you a fellow Marylander?"

"Yeah. Small world, or forest, or whatever. And the names you make up are—"

"Sucky? Yeah, I've never been much good at it." He laughs.

"I was going to say simplistic." I grin. It feels foreign to smile, like my face is cracking in half.

"Yeah, okay. But I bumped your pack and all that rolled out was that balled up sweatshirt covering something."

I tense.

He quickly adds, "I didn't touch it, I swear. And the whole point of me telling you this is because I didn't see any food. I know you're following the intuition, or I think you called it a pull?"

I rush to my pack, ignoring his rapid explanation.

"I want you to be prepared, so you should know how to hunt and you should be all stocked up." His words tumble out, embarrassed.

Nothing seems out of order. I flip open the top, but my brother is still tucked in and snug. It's not like Wyatt went rooting through my things, but I still feel stony and stiff.

I focus on the fact that he's improving my survivability in this forest, despite his odd behavior, the result of being here too long. It isn't the way I felt yesterday, either. Like he was trying to take over and show me "how it's done." He's showing me something, yes, but I feel this sense of validation. I need food, and instead of being the savior, he's going to teach me how to hunt. He's surprised at how far I've made it, and seems to believe I'm capable of learning more.

"It's fine," I say, more to reassure myself than him as I walked back over to him. "That goat boy thing, you talked about it last night?"

"The Rot?"

"Yes, he touched all my food."

"Shit!"

"Yeah. And I was so hungry. That's why I ate all those stupid berries."

"Oh, man. A similar thing happened to me, except I fed all my food to a Stain. So don't worry about that. There's no way you could have known. Just follow me over here. I want you to use this."

I almost have to jog to keep up with his excited steps. He takes me behind the branch-woven dome and shows me a mostly dried skull. It's clearly the Owletta's. The wide sockets make the skull appear surprised. The beak hooks, just as sharp as before. The top of the skull is rounded, and there's only a few bits of flesh stuck to it.

"I'm surprised. It's not as white as your skull is," I say.

"That's because it isn't sun-bleached yet, and under these thick trees, I have to add salt to it to speed up the process. I cleaned it as best I could, but I think you should use it today. The hide is just too wet right now, but this will help for sure."

He opens the beak and snaps off the bottom jaw. Wyatt places the rounded skull over mine. It fits perfectly, like a protective helmet. I thought I would find it repulsive, but when I take in the campsite through the wide eye sockets, I see Hollow Forest in a new way. I'm a part of it now, undetected. I hadn't let this creature get to me. I had survived, in more ways than one.

"Let's go," I say. "I'm hungry."

# CHAPTER TWELVE

I'm in a twisted fairytale as I'm led astride Laken around the outside of camp. Wyatt holds a roughly cut leather strap attached to a halter and keeps his eye focused on the ground. Laken's ears point back at me, listening and curious about her new rider. I take deep breaths that match the pacing of her hooves and feel the warmth of her skin through my jeans.

"This is what I'm talking about," Wyatt says, making me jolt.

Laken stomps her foot in protest at his excitement.

"Ease up, girl," Wyatt says, absentmindedly stroking her muzzle. "Okay, so anything bright, you want to stay away from. These," he points at red mushroom caps, "are definitely deadly. But this one and this one are showing up because it's about to rain."

The brownish-gray mushrooms grow close to the base of a tree. Their tops look like the folds of brains. Definitely not appetizing. He picks one up and hands it to me.

"No thanks," I have to keep myself from shoving his hand aside.

He shrugs his shoulders and eats the fungus before towing me and Laken along. He puts the other one in a sack he brought with him.

"Aha," he said, stopping again.

The Owletta skull wobbles on my head. Laken paws at the ground, eager to continue moving.

"Look at this rock right here, Angela." He puts his hands on his hips.

I try not to look down at where his dreads lay across his broad shoulders and back. Instead I refocus on the stone. "Yeah?"

"What do you notice about it?"

I sigh, wishing I was off this angry seamare and on my own two legs. I thought it would be more relaxing to not trek anymore, but instead, I'm sore and tired. "I don't know. It has moss on some of it?"

"Right you are. Great job! What else?"

He looks up at me, his eyes glistening with hope that I'll notice what he's noticing. He needs me to see what he sees. He's showing me how to get things I need on my journey. Why am I treating this like I'm back in school? As if this isn't necessary information for me to have on my trek.

"It's wet?"

"Yes! You are doing so great. It's a little wet."

He nudges it with his bare foot. The rock loosens and overturns with a clump of dirt. Laken's nostrils flare and she snorts again.

"That, right there, is a natural spring. This is called a weeping hillside. If you dig a little, you could get some water."

And sure enough, the little ditch has a slow trickle of spring water. Laken dips her head, jerking me forward, and makes gentle huffs of breath over the area.

"Atta girl," he pats her neck "that's the stuff you love."

I lean forward, trying to get a look, but he's already leading me down a different way. I hadn't noticed at first, but there are spots where the moss is thinner or tracks that have compacted mud and dirt ever so slightly. We are following worn paths that look like he's used them over and over again.

It doesn't take us long to reach a cluster of bushes and grasses. The air feels heavy and damp. My skin is sticky from the moisture and I taste the low clouds, threatening to release rain.

"You might want to get down to see this up close. If you ever need to survive off salad for a bit, you'll keep this in mind."

I get ready to dismount and my heart flutters when he comes closer, ready to assist me. I don't want him that close. I don't know him. I can't have him touching me. Where would he help me? *How* would he help me?

"I've got it," I say, the panic in my voice making Laken side-step and I fall to the ground.

She shakes her head, flipping her mane from one side of her neck to the other. My tumble only makes Wyatt come to my side faster.

"You okay?" He reaches out a hand and tries to catch my gaze as I dust myself off.

I take off the skull and keep my head low, feeling dizzy. I ignore his outstretched hand. His palms have callouses, his arms are thick, and his reach looks inviting. There's nothing I want to do more than hold it and trust him. But it's dangerous to project your wishes on someone else.

"I'm fine, but thanks." My face feels hot and I quickly put the mask back on.

"We've all had a gravity moment a time or two, especially with Laken here. She's a great beast, but she's a thing of the forest."

"Sorry," I mumble.

"No need to apologize." He walks to the bushes like nothing happened, leaving me alone with my embarrassment. "There are so many kinds of species in Hollow Forest. Some I feel mimic stuff from our world," he points a finger from me to himself, "and others are totally from here. Like Laken."

"Oh, so some are from folklore or from scripture," I say.

"What do you mean?"

"Like Laken, your 'seahorse', is probably a kelpie." He stares at me. "You met her in the lake. She tried to drown you. You gained her trust. Now she's loyal."

"Huh. I weirdly feel better knowing that there are stories behind it and a name to it. But you've gotta admit, seahorse is pretty clever."

I can't help but laugh. "Yep. All your names are clever. I think The Rot is something from folk tales too, but I can't quite remember what."

"Wow! How do you know all these things?"

I feel like such a poser when I say, "I briefly had a podcast in college where I did a few episodes about myths and legends." He looks confused. "It's like a radio show that you can listen to whenever. It was part of my senior project." There it was again. That feeling of having too many words in my mouth, too much air in my lungs, and a rush to tell him things so he knows I'm not completely clueless. I'm not dead weight.

"That is so cool. Well, to add to that, here are some chickweed, red clover, and dandelions. The dandelions are a bit bitter, but they tastes better when you know they won't kill you." He lets out a short laugh.

I cringe, wondering how he's learned to identify these plants. I hope it's from his time outside of here, not from personal experience.

"And this, here, touch this leaf." He holds out a branch from a taller bush.

My hand brushes his as I hold the leaf in my fingers. The top is flat and a light green while the bottom has thin, clear fuzz, as soft as peach skin. He's so close to me that his arm accidentally bumps mine. I have to let go and take a step back to get away from the electric tingling against my forearm.

"Sorry about that. Here, I'll just pluck one off." He holds it in front of us. "You can eat as much of this as you want. If I make myself a forest salad, I use mostly these leaves and add some other blooms and stems to taste. I honestly don't have to eat or sleep that much. I can go without if I need to, but you're going to need to know how to find this stuff because you need it every day." With that, he pops it in his mouth and chews happily.

"So I can just eat it, right like this?"

He nods.

I squirm at the images of unwashed lettuce, but I'm roughing it now. How else am I expecting to eat? I take off a leaf and slowly chew. It tastes crisp and clean. Maybe it's because I'm starving, or maybe it's because I realize that it's probably not salmonella that would kill me here, but I eat a few more.

"You've got it," he says. He looks relieved that I've eaten something.

There's a cold splat on my head and the leaves twist and turn in a chilled breeze. There's a looming, gray cloud visible through the branches. More droplets fall from the sky and Wyatt hurries to put some greens in his knapsack. Rain collects and drips from the canopy. There's a rush of wind that whips as the branches sway. There's a whisper to it. The pull pulses within me and I stare in that direction. My arm jerks to the side and my eyes flutter.

"You're feeling it, huh?" Wyatt grows still.

"Yeah," I say.

"Maybe once you learn some more, you can be on your way."

Was he kicking me out? Am I overstaying my welcome? He's

the one who told me to follow him. I wasn't the one luring people to my camp.

He must notice how conflicted I am because he says, "I want to make sure you're prepared before you keep following that, what do you call it? The pull? Definitely don't rush it. I'll make sure you have all you need."

Jessica said that I shouldn't ignore it. But I'm so exhausted, so unprepared. Was it a bad choice to follow Wyatt's lead? And what was I supposed to do now? Just walk into the woods without my stuff? I think on it and decide that I'm returning to his camp.

There's something about the way he moves that makes me stiffen. I can't place my finger on it, but it was too quick, too secretive. I whip around to look at him and he puts a finger to his lips. I tremble, not knowing what's happening. He ducks a little lower and Laken bobs her head down with him. I crouch and look where he's pointing.

Through the branches of the shrubs and grasses I see what looks like a giant deer. It's beautiful in the quick wind that ruffles its fur. It sniffs the air and I get a pit in my stomach. I'm glad we are downwind of it. I wanted it to be normal. I wanted to just say, "So what, it's just a deer." But I knew it wasn't just a deer, just like Laken isn't just a horse and Wyatt isn't just a man.

"That's a Ruminant," Wyatt dared whisper. "A blood-fed Ruminant."

I shiver.

"I can kill it if I have to," he unsheaths one of his knives, "but I'd rather just not mess with it. Don't bother it and *hopefully* it won't bother you."

It lowers its head. Is it prowling? Its movements are slow, smooth, and graceful. It looks like it glides among the ferns and moss, and then it strikes. Its antlers swing and fling some kind of furry creature that hisses and growls into the air. The creature tries to escape, but the Ruminant flicks back its head, as if its neck is broken. Rows of teeth and mouths within mouths slurp and salivate. Its antlers crack forward like mandibles and entrap the creature, holding it hostage before it can limp away. The prey has to face the rows of teeth.

I have to look away. I can't watch that thing in its last moments before it has to endure the Ruminant's jaws. Instead, I turn to Wyatt, who's worried yet deeply concentrated. He can't seem to take his eyes off the scene. He's tense and ready to pounce and protect if need be.

It's over quickly even though I feel like I've been squatting forever. Wyatt raises slightly to watch the Ruminant, now stained with blood, leap away as if it hadn't just tortured an animal.

"I guess it got enough to fill its four stomachs," he said, his mouth tight in a grimace.

How would he know that it had four stomachs? And then I make the connection. His headware. He's had to face one of them before. The skull that looked like a deer was actually one of these blood-fed Ruminants. Bile builds up in my throat, and I swallow it down.

"I think we should head back to camp. It looks like it's gonna rain and we've seen enough for today."

He tries to help me back on Laken, but I don't let him close and I can't get up on my own, even when I use a nearby rock as a stepping stool. So he teaches me to lead Laken. She tests me a few times by jerking her head or refusing to move, but Wyatt shows me how to stand and where to face to be a better team with her. We make it back to the tree line and as Wyatt knocks three times on each twin tree, I feel Hollow Forest call to me. It whispers in my ears.

# CHAPTER THIRTEEN

"Come on, just push off of the log onto Laken's back," Wyatt encourages.

The antlers of his Ruminant mask sway as Laken prances, anxious to move. The Ruminant hide is tied around his shoulders and drapes over Laken's back. It has deer-like, brown fur that spikes up in a few places.

"I thought you said you've ridden before. And you did great on your own yesterday. We just need to go a bit further this time."

I think back to the leisurely seaside trail ride I went on for my sixteenth birthday. The trail leader said that my horse, Heck, was the "grandpa" of the group at a whopping twenty-seven years old. We strode at about one mile per hour, leagues behind the other horses. My mom, dad, and Donny had all been way off in the distance while Heck wanted to take a nap standing up by the waves. I didn't blame him. It was relaxing.

"Not like this. Where's the saddle?" I ask. I thought yesterday was just a leisurely scavenge where he hadn't felt like putting on a saddle for such a brief time out of camp.

"You don't need one. You can feel the muscle movements better this way, anyway," he says. "Look, I'm holding her steady.

I just need you to grab either her mane or my arm or something, and swing your right leg over her back so you can sit on down here." He pats the spot in front of him. "Then I'll be kind of like a seatbelt and I'll hold the reins while you hold her mane."

"It sounds complicated." I equally felt nervous about having him that close and yet comforted. What would it be like to have his arms surround me? My cheeks feel warm.

"It's really not, and we need to get going." He tries to keep the curtness of his voice even as his hands tighten on the reins.

There's a pressure in my chest. "We could walk. Can she even see?"

"First of all, that would take forever. Second of all, Laken sees in different ways than us. You'll be surprised. Come on. I know you can do it."

I hold my breath and launch myself onto Laken. I push off too hard. My stomach lurches as the world tilts and the ground veers toward me as I start to fall off the other side. I scramble to stay on. My launching act startles Laken. She prances in place, her shoulders knocking the wind out of my gut and her bare skin sticking to mine. As I sit up, Wyatt steadies me. I flinch from his touch on my waist and he yanks his hand off me. We both nervously straighten our skull masks and situate ourselves. I grow hot with his chest occasionally bumping against my shoulder blades.

"See, not so bad," he says. "Just grab onto her mane."

I grab a handful of her dark, gray, coarse hair. "Does this hurt her? Holding her hair like this?" I push down Jacob's phantom hand stroking my hair and focus on Wyatt's forearms. They're tense, yet gentle on Laken's lead.

"Not at all. Their bangs, or forelock, has more nerve endings, but her crest, which is the hair along her neck here, doesn't have much feeling in it. You're doing great. But you need to relax your legs more. You're spooking her."

I sigh and my muscles relax in my legs. Laken relaxes, too.

"Don't I need to hold on with my legs?" I ask.

"I mean, not really. It's more of a balance thing." He turns her to the right. "You make the left rein looser and gently direct her with the right. Like this."

Laken turns on a dime. I shift my weight so I don't fall off. It's more comfortable when I get the rhythm as she plods on. I'm definitely a better rider than I was yesterday, but maybe that's me being overconfident. Our legs sway like pendulums. My machete bounces gently against my thigh. On the way out of camp we take the same zig-zagging pattern, knocking three times on each of the trees with matching symbols. Layers of fog lift like last night. The winding path is free of those diamond symbols, so Laken won't get scorched.

"This confuses the Fiends, the things that are preying on us. It makes my home almost invisible with the fog. Then, if they do happen to find it, they've got the Fiend screens to try and run through, and they'll get singed until they're dead. Like one big bug light. One time I didn't know I was being stalked, and a Rot ran in there and they fried so bad, their eyes popped." He laughs. "Just popped right out there and melted."

His chest rises and falls with his laughter and makes me sick. He's been here too long.

"I'm glad you set up this system," I say, swallowing.

"I have lots of hacks here. There's clay I dug up from The Mount across the lake where I got Laken and brought it here. For some reason, Fiends can make themselves invisible. But, when they set foot on that clay, that's when they're made to show themselves, no matter what. It's like a detecting trap."

Laken walks silently through the forest. She moves through the trees with ease. Wyatt's right. She senses in her own way. She doesn't have to be led. Each step she takes is purposeful and sure.

"See the clay patches around the perimeter? It's the orangey stuff."

"Yeah. It's the same as the powder you put on the Owletta hide," I say.

"Yep! It makes sure that the hide stays visible and dries it out. You're a quick learner."

I can't help but be prideful as we ride deeper into the Hollow. I focus on moving with Laken. Her wide, strong back makes it easier to find my balance. Her mane feels like I'm holding a clump of straw. It's mesmerizing to sway with Laken's steps and her muted footfalls. We walk through lone rays of light and over fallen rotten trees.

There are taps and clicks in the distance, ones that I've heard before. Ones that meant something was trying to interfere. I think back to when I'd get the zap click on my calls and a breath catches in my throat. Laken's skin twitches.

"Try not to tense up," Wyatt says in an instructor's voice.

I keep my breathing even, focusing on the in and out. Focusing on the fact that I have more or less of a team now. I'm not completely alone. Not like I was with that book Donny brought home. I can still remember the first time I was alone with it.

Donny went to get more candles or sage and left his book in the middle of the living room floor. It was so unassuming. It was just a book, flipped open to his favorite page. There wasn't an anarchy symbol, upside-down cross, or anything like that. No circle of crystals, though he used his fair share of those, too. Just a book with words. Harmless. I could easily rip out pages, shred it, burn it, drown it.

And every ounce of myself wanted to tear it apart, to dropkick that thing across the room. I wanted it out of my house, out of this town, off the Earth. But I couldn't move an inch toward it. I could only stare and hope that it would spontaneously combust. I felt like electricity was running through my spine, propelling me forward to just do it. My heart beat wildly in my chest. Just. Get. Rid of it.

I almost jumped out of my skin when my brother unlocked the door and swung it open, whistling. He just left a minute ago. How had he come home so fast with a shitton of sage?

"You're back?"

"Yeah."

It was surprising to me that he didn't know how rattled I was. I tried to compose myself and act as if I wasn't trying to destroy the one bright spot of happiness he had in his world.

"Were you taking a break from work?" he asked.

"It's Saturday," I said. I was sick of avoiding everything and just doing overtime for work. All Mom and Dad ever did was ignore or get rid of the stuff they didn't agree with. I didn't want to do that anymore.

"I'm sure you have some calls to get to, though. You did that last weekend," Donny said, a slight panic creeping into his voice.

"Nope, not this week. I thought I'd take the weekend off."

His eyes darkened, but he didn't say anything. I held my breath and searched for signs of his anger. But he gave his head a little shake. "Well, maybe Zach won't be shy this time. Maybe he'll want to talk to you."

"Why wouldn't he want to talk to me? Zach knows me. I let you guys stay in my dorm."

"I don't know what to tell you, Ange. He's appreciative of your hospitality. He really is. He just says that you don't really get it, sometimes."

"My hospitality?"

"You know what I mean. Like he's glad, and I'm glad, too, that you still love me even though Mom and Dad don't. He just thinks you don't understand certain things. Like, basically, your judgments get in the way of our communication, and he doesn't want to talk with your negative energy around."

My hands clench into fists. "My negative energy?"

"Don't get offended. I don't think you're negative, but with you trying to convince me to stop talking to Zach, well, it hurts."

"You talk to him like eight to ten hours a day!" My voice was louder than I wanted it to be.

"It used to be more than that, Ange. We lived together. I was saving up for—"

For drugs. He was always saving up for more drugs.

"A ring. He was my soulmate."

I wanted to gag.

"You don't really get close to people, Angelita. So you just don't understand."

I wanted to scream at him. I opened my mouth, but no words came out, so my jaw hung open.

"I know why. I get it. It makes total sense with what happened to you, but just don't try and separate us. Try to keep an open mind and imagine how I'm feeling after losing someone I'm in love with."

Try to keep an open mind? I was the only reason he wasn't living on the street right now. Why was he warping what was going on? He was so damn selfish. My spite fueled me to take the weekend off. I'd been too accommodating, which is why I was getting walked all over. Donny needed limits. He was so all or nothing. When he wanted to work out, he took steroids and starved himself. When he wanted to be in a relationship, he attached himself to that person. When he wanted to speak to the dead, he'd do it 24/7. It was exhausting, and I wasn't going to let him or his dead boyfriend push me around.

I wasn't hovering over him or anything, but I certainly wasn't going to make it easy for them to talk, either. I kept my door open. I blasted music and rearranged my fluffy pillows on my bed. I vacuumed and dusted. He must have tried moving things around and repeating himself a hundred times. After about three episodes of *Will and Grace's* live audience-recorded laughter ricocheted off the apartment walls, he showed up in the doorway to my room.

"He's not talking." His lips were pressed so hard together, they formed a white line.

"He said he won't talk to you?"

"No, he's not talking at all," he snapped.

I didn't back down. I stared right back.

"I'm sorry, it just feels like I lost him all over again, you know," Donny said.

According to Selfish Don, I didn't know..

"I'll try again tomorrow, but I don't think it'll work today," he whispered, more to himself than to me. "Maybe I just need some rest."

And that's how we spent our Saturday, with Donny descending back into Depressionland, and me trying to stay firm and distract myself with sitcoms.

I constantly had to remind myself why it was better this way and fought the tiny voice in my head saying that I was being self-centered. Instead, I focused on how pleased I was with my backbone, that is until nighttime rolled around. I was brushing my teeth when Don's stiff body stood in the doorway.

"Yeah," I said, with toothpaste leaking out of my mouth in thick, foamy drops.

He didn't say anything. So I spit, feeling myself get defensive. After I rinsed my mouth out, I tried to leave, but somehow Don made his entire waif of a body fill up the doorway. I glared at him.

"Excuse you."

"I wanted to talk to Zach today," he said, coolly.

"No one was stopping you."

"Well, actually, one person was."

"I don't know what to tell you. I can't work every day of the week. I need a break."

"Do you, though?" He gave that half-smile with no teeth. He took a step forward and bumped his chest into mine.

He didn't bump me hard, but I wasn't expecting it, either. I fell backward right on my ass. It didn't hurt me, not physically. Don loomed over me. His lip curled and his frame was stiff. I sat there with my mouth gaping, unable to form words.

"Talking to people is good for you. It would help you, I think. So, why don't you get some overtime talking to people at your work."

It wasn't a suggestion.

I finally got ahold of myself, at least a little bit, and with shivering limbs, used the toilet to pull myself up. My arms and legs felt like lead. I looked at my brother right in his smirking face.

"Or, you could not push me around, and be grateful you even have a place to stay," I said.

"What. Are you going to kick me out? You wouldn't do that to your *brother*." He took a sudden step forward again, but this time I was ready.

I put my hands on his thin chest and shoved as hard as I could. His rigid body gave way to my thrust, and he fell backward out of my tiny bathroom. He hit the wall, hard.

He didn't fall all the way down like I did, but he got the idea. His eyes rolled and showed their whites before he balanced himself and blinked at me. "What the fuck, Ange? If I was in your way, just say so. Good God!"

"Don't touch me again." My voice hitched.

He straightened himself out, threw his hands up, and walked back to the living room.

"And I'm not working overtime tomorrow, you hear me? I deserve time off, and you need a break from your stupid dead boyfriend!"

"Okay," he yelled from the living room. "Chill the fuck out, Ange."

My chest heaved and my hands clenched and unclenched into fists. Maybe if he spent more time job searching, then he wouldn't be such a fucking waste of space that I had to take care of. I wasn't going to get pushed around, literally, by anyone. Tears spilled down my cheeks and a knot formed in my stomach. How could I think those things? Donny was a good man, a good brother, and needed support. Why would I mentally repeat the things he's heard his whole life? Why wouldn't I expect that he'd go hard with this thing that made him feel connected?

I changed into my pajamas. I've been disappointed and overwhelmed with Donny before, but this was the first time I thought about kicking Donny out. Some close friends from college would occasionally message or Skype me and ask how it was going with my brother. I would always tell them that it was tough sometimes, but definitely worth being there for my brother's recovery. They'd tell me, "Oh Angela, I could never do what you do." I always thought, that's what the Soloman siblings did for each other. He already had been abandoned so many times, by my parents, by "friends", and by his exes.

Even those times I caught him rifling through stuff in my room to sell, or the times he was trying to hide that he was high, I never thought that he needed to be kicked out or that I couldn't handle his recovery process. If anything, it reaffirmed that he needed to live with me, in my apartment, away from predators, and be a part of my boring life. I would be his support. I would have his back. But if he was going to touch me like that, maybe I was wrong. There needed to be limits.

Wyatt's voice jolts me out of my memory. "Okay, I'm going to pick up speed. Don't tense up. Even I can feel that you're not relaxing. Take a breath and go with Laken's movements." Laken's ears rotated back when she hears her name. "I don't want you to be afraid of going a little faster."

He clicks his tongue and leans forward. She picks up pace. My butt bounces against her back. My teeth gnash together.

"Relax your legs and point your toes up."

I do and my butt stays moving with her. Instead, my legs bounce like shock absorbers. We ride like this until Wyatt leans forward a little more. I follow his lead. He squeezes his legs again, and she picks up the pace. I make myself breathe as I rise and fall. My hips scoop in circles.

"Lean forward more. You're doing great." His words of encouragement and the snapping of my ratty hair whip in my ears.

I lean into the rhythm, allowing the air to whoosh past me. It feels like we're going a million miles per hour. Laken continues to charge, her breathing steady, everything moving in a pattern. A laugh bubbles out of me and a little scream escapes my lips. It makes Laken pick up more speed.

Foliage and branches dance when we rush past. Birds call overhead while creatures just out of view scratch and scurry away from her thunderous hooves. It feels like we are part of a moving pattern. We're a wave amongst Fiends and the energy of the dark, leafy forest. Mud splatters as we pass through puddles and sticks snap as she runs over them.

"Easy there, Laken." Wyatt pulls back slightly on the reins.

She slows to the bouncing gate and then to a brisk walk. "We have to cut your hair better, or tie it back or something." He laughs. "It keeps slapping me in the face."

"Sorry." I can't stop giggling. "How did you get so good at this? Aren't you from Baltimore?"

"I said I was born in Baltimore. I'm from West Virginia. Wild and Wonderful. I grew up on a farm with my mom and dad."

"You're just full of secrets," I say.

"I'm telling you everything I know," he says, surprised.

"Not your full name."

"Shh, look," he says.

All three of us stiffen and I turn in the direction of where he's pointing. There's a giant, wild rabbit. It's the size of a Great Dane. It has gazelle-like horns that spiral straight up. It has to be a Jackalope.

"It's huge," I whisper.

Its long ears flick in our direction and it sniffs the air. Six black eyes, three on each side set vertically on top of one another, fixate on us.

"It's gonna run at us," Wyatt says, squaring us up to face it. We're watching it head-on.

"What? Are we going to joust?" I hiss.

"Kind of. Relax your muscles and hold on." He clicks his tongue.

The Jackalope lowers its chin to its chest and bounds forward, twirled antlers jutting right at us. We lope toward it. Laken snorts and Wyatt whips out one of his black knives. He leans far forward, pushing me to lean as well. When we are a breath apart, Wyatt tilts his body ever so slightly and we veer to the side, allowing his low-hanging knife to be at the beast's neck level. His upper body tenses around me.

There's a crack and Wyatt curses under his breath. The black knife flies through the air. Its antlers must have knocked it out of his hands. The Jackalope turns swiftly and thumps its foot. It lowers its head again.

"You try it with your blade," Wyatt says.

"What? Don't you have another one?"

"Yeah, but you need to try it. These guys are aggressive, but Laken will get out of the way. Get ready."

I pull my machete out of the sheath on my hip. It slides out easily, shining silver in the dark woods. The Jackalope thumps again. It's not a warning, but a threat.

"You ready?" he asks while Laken paws and snorts. She prances and I tense. "Take a breath, relax, and hold it low. Go for under its jaw."

I don't want to go after a bunny's throat. But as we charge forward, it's clear it really isn't a bunny. It has six, black, menacing eyes. Its antlers are set to spear us. We get closer and I shut my eyes. My wrist turns the blade in the opposite direction. I try to force it forward, to make it point at our prey. When we are about to slam into the Jackalope, the machete swings up and over my shoulder, piercing Wyatt in the neck.

"No!" I scream.

Mist billows around me and I turn to him. Laken turns in response to my shift of weight and we both fall off her back. I land on my side. The wind is knocked out of my lungs and Laken's retreating hooves kick dirt in my face. I groan as I let go of the machete and try to sit up. Wyatt's right behind me, breathing hard.

"Shit! I forgot to ask its name." He chokes up mist.

Fog pours out of the side of his neck, gushing like blood would. It settles along the ground, pooling in low clouds around him.

Why hadn't I just said no and refused to do it? Or at the very least told Wyatt its name. For someone who is acting like such a know-it-all, it seems like a pretty stupid mistake not to ask. A jagged pain rakes through my ribs when I'm reminded at what a pushover I was with Donny. I was easily pressured then, and I'm angry with myself and with Wyatt for pressuring me into something before I'm ready.

"It's Totto," I say, tears welling in my eyes.

The rabbit thumps its foot again. Laken isn't in sight.

"Like the dog?" He smiles and mist spills between his teeth.

"No, like Georgia O'Keeffe's middle name," I say, not smiling back.

"Don't look," he burps out clouds of fog. The wound in his neck grows larger. His skin fades into nothingness. "Don't look at me like that. I'll come back; I just don't know when. I don't die," he says, his voice merely a whisper.

His eyes see nothing. His face and one of his shoulders disappear.

"Wyatt?" I scream at the headless body in front of me, rolling into clouds.

The rabbit doesn't wait. I'm alone and it charges.

# CHAPTER FOURTEEN

THE JACKALOPE'S HORNS point right at me as it bounds forward. I crawl to Totto, clutch it tightly, and scramble to a standing position. I bounce from foot to foot, Totto slipping in my sweaty grip. I'm not closing my eyes this time.

It jumps straight at me and I crouch to plunge Totto into its chest. With a screech that's too high for its massive body, it tries to bolt away from my stab and Totto rips from my grip. The beast falls to its side and slides. Totto is stuck fast at the end of a long gash that starts at its neck and stretches to its chest. I run toward its fallen body. I feel queasy about how I've harmed this animal – that is, until it stands and shakes itself off. It whips around, long front teeth bared. Totto remains pierced through its chest and the creature's six black eyes glare at me in pain.

A scream echoed through the forest as Laken comes galloping back. She charges at the Jackalope and slides to a halt when she rears at the beast. She brings her hooves down, hard. Its rib cage crushes and cracks when she strikes. I stay where I am when her lips peel back over her sharp teeth. Every one of them are pointed and glisten with saliva. She dives at its neck to bite, pull, and tear until she whips her head back with its throat in her mouth. She tosses it aside. Blood drips from her muzzle and down her pink chest. She screams and snorts.

"Laken," I whisper. "Shh, Laken. Easy."

She prances, dancing around her kill. When she snorts, a cloud of red mist flies out of her nostrils. She froths pink foam from her mouth. Her skin quivers and she pounces again. Her muscles tense and bulge. Her lungs heave.

"Laken, easy." I try to match Wyatt's soothing tone from before.

I take a hesitant step toward her, my hand outstretched. She whips her head to face me. Her milky eyes see nothing. Her dark gray mane is wild and sweaty. I withdraw my hand when she snaps at it. She mutilates the rabbit, throwing chunks of its furry flesh and strewing its organs. She doesn't stop until almost all of its intestines are on the outside of its body. She sighs and lowers her head, letting her muzzle drag along the length of its corpse. From the tip of its long ears all the way to its fluff tail she huffs. She paws at it and faces me.

"We have to take that back, I guess," I say.

I keep my eye on her as I grab its feet. It has to be close to a hundred pounds. I drag it a bit, but then drop it. Where the fuck are we? We hadn't gone far though, right? And I don't feel the pull. Panic presses on my chest as I dislodge Totto and tuck the machete back on my side.

I don't want to end up like that blonde girl I met when I first walked through the gate. I search wildly for something familiar but can't spot anything. The trees all look the same and yet new and different. Are they shifting? Laken meanders over to where Wyatt's hazy body is still fading away and lays down, tucking her legs under her muscular core. All that's left are his feet. She rests her muzzle on his disembodied lower limbs and sighs. She faces away from me, but her ears rotate, attentive to what I'm doing.

"What, so you're lost, too? You're just going to lay down?" I grab the legs again.

Weren't rabbits' feet supposed to be lucky? I have a giant one in each hand, Goddammit! Even though I pull with all my strength, I manage to only roll it on its side. Its guts make me gag. Only Wyatt's calloused feet are left in the rolling mist. His fog carpets the earth. Laken mourns surrounded by his cloud, giving her an ethereal look. I pull the rabbit as hard as I can, slowly walking backward. Its crushed skull and front paws drag. My foot catches on a root and I slip and fall right on my ass.

Anger wells inside me. I'm lost. I don't have intuition. I stabbed a poor, wild animal. Wyatt turned into a fucking cloud. And now, Laken's rabid. How are we supposed to bring this back, anyway? Maybe I'm supposed to put it on Laken's back and we're going to walk it to Wyatt's branch dome. I get myself up with a groan, brush off the leaves that cling to my clothes, and pick up its feet again.

I drag it until I'm next to Laken. I lay it parallel to her, despite her objective snorts. I stand on the other side of her, reach over her broad back, grab its legs, and strain to drag it over her.

She jolts up, forcing me to slip off her. She turns sharply and faces her rump to me. I jump out of the way as she kicks. I can't tell if she intended to strike me or wanted to warn me off. Either way, she wants me to stop bothering her while she pines for Wyatt. She gets comfortable again next to his body, tucking in her legs and resting her muzzle on what's left of him, which are just several toes at this point.

The golden light is dimming behind the canopy. I don't want to be left out here again, aimless, with no pull or guide. Only the encroaching darkness to look forward to. How does Wyatt do this all the time? Hunt and live off the land with only a horse and a bird? And then it hits me. Skeletor.

I whistle.

And wait.

Nothing.

I scream his name into Hollow Forest, desperation leaks into my voice.

Nothing.

I clap my hands.

Nothing.

I whistle again.

That's when he dives.

He's been as silent as the night. He swoops down, making me jump to the side, and launches back into the air with the Jackalope, that's at least 100 pounds, gripped in his talons. As he flaps, the guts swing in the air. He's flying back to camp and I can't lose him.

"Laken, come on. He said he'd come back. Okay? We've got to go."

She remains saddened and ignores me. I snatch up Wyatt's pelt and tie his Ruminant skull around my waist. I carefully walk to Laken, trying to get closer while avoiding her potential strikes. I saw what she did to that rabbit.

She lays her ears back flat against her head and bares her sharp teeth at me again.

"No. Don't you show your teeth at me. We are going back to your home. We are making it. We're not going to sulk. If you stay still while you grieve, you will get lost. And we. Are. Not. Staying. Lost," I say, throwing the pelt on her back like a blanket.

I plopped myself on her back before she comes at me. There's no way I'll keep up with that vulture on foot. Her ears stay flat against her head and she refuses to get up. I try kicking my feet and she just snorts. It doesn't work, anyway. I can barely squeeze my legs around her broad back. I stick my tongue to the roof of my mouth and pull in air from the side to finally get my tongue to do that clicking noise.

She straightens her front legs and I have to clutch her mane and reins so I won't slide right off her hindquarters. She straightens her back legs and shakes. Somehow I manage to remain locked to her. I let the left rein go slack like Wyatt taught me, and ever so gently pull the right. It works. She turns. Not happily, but it works.

I click again and almost fly right off when she takes off running like an asshole. I make myself breathe, relax, and lean into the wind. We cut through the forest. Her hooves pound against the earth as she avoids fallen trees and rocks with ease. Skeletor isn't too far ahead of us. It isn't until I see patches of the ruddy clay that I'm relieved.

"Easy." Laken slows to a bouncing trot, then a walk. I move with her to the first pair of trees with the triangular symbols and Skeletor disappears into the fog above the camp.

# CHAPTER FIFTEEN

I TRY TO sleep that night after prepping the kill as best I can, but constant thoughts of if, where, and when Wyatt would return made my skull feel like it would crack open. What did he even mean by "come back" anyway? Would he be a bunch of misty particles? What if I breathe him in by accident and he won't be able to reanimate or whatever? But that doesn't make any sense. Needless to say, I don't get any sleep that first night.

There's nothing I can do. Nothing I can change. I'm helpless in this unforgiving world. I feel a cold fear like a heavy rock in the pit of my stomach. It's exactly how I felt on that awful night with Don.

That same night Don shoved me, I woke up in my apartment around 3:00 A.M. from a nightmare. I couldn't remember exactly what it was about, but fear coursed through me. With clammy skin and no breath left in my lungs, I sat straight up, fighting the descent back into terror. With enough time, my brain would cook up something else to entertain me while I sleep.

I was about to lay back down when I heard something. I rubbed my eyes and ears to get rid of the remnants of my bad dream. It was still there. Someone was talking. If Donny invited friends over, he was absolutely out of here. He knew that was one of the rules. He could see whatever drug-dealing assholes he wanted, but they absolutely were not allowed into my home. I stood up and went to the edge of my room to hover in the door-way. I held my breath.

"That's what . . . And I tried . . . ." There were bits and pieces of what I thought was Donny whispering in a fast, breathy tone.

"Not well enough," said a smooth voice. The voice wasn't whispering, but yet it was intimate. It was like they were right next to you, keeping their voice low and talking to you in bed.

"Why would . . .? Not enough . . . isn't my . . . ."

"It's not up for discussion," said the cool voice.

Did Donny owe someone money or something? What if a creep found out where we lived and came here? Or what if some-one was going to try and get to me to get to Donny? I crept out to the edge of the kitchen so I could listen better.

Donny's voice began to waver. "I can't do that. I could never do that."

I peered through the opening into the living room. Donny was wringing his hands and standing up against the wall. His toes were against the baseboard. Who else was speaking?

"You have to. Don't you want to speak to Zach again?" said the voice.

Dread washed over me like ice. The smooth voice was coming from Don.

"No, he's dead. I'm over him now," Donny said fiercely, in his own voice. I could tell he was crying.

"Come now. Don't lie to yourself," it said.

And that's when Don whipped around and stared right at me. His eyes, usually sparkly and a vibrant black, glinted at me, making my heart pound. "*You*," said the cold voice.

I stumbled backward. Donny shook his head, and he looked scared. His eyebrows were furrowed and tears streamed down his cheeks. "I'm so sorry, Angelita. I was so wrong. It wasn't Zach," he choked. "Run."

Don stiffened and sneered at me. His teeth gleamed in what little light streamed into the apartment. His shoulders were tight and hunched as he ran straight for me. His movements too fluid. I slipped on the carpeting at first but got enough traction to run back to my bedroom. I tried to slam the door in Don's face, but whatever it was flew in on me, flinging me backward. I grabbed at anything so I wouldn't fall. Instead, I gripped my comforter from my bed and got entangled as I hit the floor.

Don rushed at me faster than he's ever moved. He clutched my neck and squeezed. My breath caught, and my eyes felt like they were going to pop out of my skull. I thrashed and twisted, but I only managed to get even more caught. My fingers and toes tingled. My head throbbed. My mind repeated the words, "This isn't real. This isn't real. This isn't real," over and over again.

Don's vice-like hold on my neck wasn't nearly as scary as his face. He was grinning. And this time, it wasn't the smirky half-smile. This time, it showed all his teeth. They gleamed, white and shiny in my dark bedroom. He leaned in closer, his nose inches from mine. His eyes were wickedly gleeful and glinted as they wished for my death. He wasn't letting go. I couldn't see this thing as my brother.

I kicked with all the strength I had. I used my fingernails to claw at his face. I couldn't tell if I was making any headway until my knee hit his gut. It didn't stop him from strangling me, but it made him loosen his grip, just a little, and that's all I needed.

I jerked my head forward and smash him in the nose with my forehead. He reeled back as I gasped for breath. I used my feet to pedal-kick my comforter and him both into a tangled wad. That thing hissed as it fought to get the covers off. I rolled onto my hands and knees, coughing and choking. I puked as I tried to stand on my feet, but fell back down to my knees, too oxygen-deprived to stand up.

While still snared in my comforter, that thing crawled. It raked at the air between us, desperate to get me. I grabbed anything I could and found myself clasping a flip flop. With a slap, I whacked it across its face and then fell onto my hands again in a coughing fit. Black spots dotted my vision. Its head cracked to the side, stunned, but it hadn't stopped.

"Get out of my house," I rasped.

It crawled toward me again, with more speed and determination.

I grabbed again and my hands found my lamp. I swung at it. "Leave," *thunk*, one hit on its forehead "us," another clocked its eye, "alone!" I screamed and threw the whole motherfucking lamp at its face.

Its head flicked back from the blows. We froze for a second before it sat back on its haunches, sighing. I used my end-table to steady myself as I shakily got to my feet. It stared at me again. Its hands flew up to its mouth and its eyes grew wide.

"Oh my God," it whispered and started walking on its knees toward me.

"No," I screamed.

"Angelita, it's okay. It's me."

"Stop." I sobbed and choked. My neck throbbed.

"Ange, it's gone." Donny reached his hand out as if I was a feral animal he was trying to catch. "I don't know when it will be back, but I think you hurt it or something."

I couldn't do this. I wouldn't do this. What if it was just

tricking me like how it tricked Donny into talking to "Zach"? I scurried onto my bed and then catapulted myself past my brother and out of the bedroom. I ran toward the front door, tears blinding my vision.

"Angelita, wait!" Donny called.

I didn't look back.

"I'm sorry."

I slammed the door behind me. I ran in my bare feet and pajamas to somewhere else, anywhere but that Hell.

The funny thing was that I ran from that nightmare only to wind up in another. There's a weight to the Hollow's darkness, a chill of helplessness, and a pressure to figure this shit out before it's too late. How long did I have before I'd no longer be able to "release Donny's essence"? A month, maybe? A few weeks? I spend the night listening to the clicks and snaps in the woods while my memory echoes the ghostly image of Don's white, glistening teeth in the blackness that surrounds me. I scramble to my backpack and yank my brother out.

I hold him close, wishing he was here to make me feel better like how he used to when I was a kid. Like how he used to make up stories when I was in elementary school so I'd sleep. Like how he threatened to beat up the guy who bullied me after I rejected him. How he used to paint my nails and do my hair after I'd go through a breakup. When he'd be more himself and want to watch movies with me or just talk. Back before everything got so fucked-up. I grasp Donny in my arms and rock, waiting for just a little light to show itself.

# CHAPTER SIXTEEN

THE NEXT DAY is unsettling. There's a practically flattened carcass of that large rabbit just lying there like a rug because Skeletor has eaten all its bones. Laken has ripped apart some of its skin and is eating its back leg. When I walk closer, she bares her sharp teeth as my stomach grumbles. It isn't until she has her fill that she allows me to eat.

I don't want to eat raw meat. My mind conjures images of intestinal worms and parasites. And can meat sit out like that all night, even though I put salt on it? Jessica made it very clear that I can't use false light or make fires. She said something about it being a beacon or something that draws unwanted attention. But I'm desperate and want to test it while I'm safe in the camp. I guess Jessica is right for once, or maybe I'm just a sucky fire starter, because I can't get even a spark. I use Totto to clean as much of the skin off as I can. I bite into the leg and almost spit it out. Too much salt. But my starving stomach makes me tear into a couple more bites before I feel nauseous.

During the next few days, I sit around and sip on the water supply we have left and take little bites from our kill. I try to make it last between us. Sometimes Skeletor flies away and I feel this weight of loss so great I burst into tears. He always comes back a few hours later with a femur or skull in his talons. He drops them on a stump or a rock in the camp, shatters it, and swallows the splintered pieces whole.

I try to be constructive and forage for more moss to add to the bedding close to camp. No pull calls to me, leaving me directionless and relying on the scavenging tactics Wyatt taught me. I practice getting on and off Laken when she finds it in her cold heart to tolerate my struggles to mount and dismount. I ride her around the camp's clearing, afraid I'll lose her in the forest. I find a way to make a little running jump, grab her mane, lean forward, and swing my right leg over her back. It isn't with grace or ease, but I do it. And for the most part, Laken is getting used to me.

I find a slow, trickling spring close by and when we run out of water, I take my empty gallon and the water skins and fill them a few times to bring as much liquid back as I can. Laken always swallows greedily. She sometimes knocks it out of my hands and spills the water on the ground. She lies in it with a groan, her skin thirsting for submersion. Skeletor leaves us at times. He can obviously care for himself. But Laken is getting sicker and sicker. Her skin becomes dry, pale, and scaly. Her pallor is yellow and gray instead of pink and dappled. I need Wyatt to come back.

That's probably how Donny felt when I left him that night and ran away. All he must have wanted was for me to come back. I ran until I got to a 7-Eleven. I never thought I'd be so happy to see its half-lit sign and loiterers joking with each other in clouds of exhaled smoke. I opened the glass door and ignored the notice that clearly stated that I needed shoes for service. The fluorescent lighting and stale air were welcomed. I wandered, letting my feet peel with each step on the sticky floor. I opened the suctioned door where the drinks were kept to feel that blast of cold air. It reminded me I was a real person. The clerk demanded I buy something or get out, but I couldn't bring myself to leave, so I pretended I was looking for the absolute perfect beef jerky while the clerk eyeballed me. It wasn't until I saw the first signs of the morning sunrise that I felt somewhat okay to venture out of the store. I trekked back to my apartment. My aching throat was a reminder of what I ran from just a few short hours ago.

I stood outside of my apartment for at least thirty minutes and tried to control my breathing. My hand loosely gripped the knob and my forehead rested against the door. The birds sang and cars rumbled past, containing people who were on their way to work or school. I felt this pulsing anger extend throughout my body. How could things continue as usual when I had just been attacked by a monster? How could birds sing and people just get up and go to work when my brother tried to kill me? Didn't they know that people couldn't be helped? That they were all just one wrong turn away from tragedy and heartache?

Should I call the police? And tell them what? That my brother had been talking to a book? That I watched him lose control of his sanity and kept trudging forward to prove to everyone that my brother could be redeemed? That he isn't a killer? But he already did kill someone once. I shuddered, not wanting something waiting for me, lurking in my apartment. I hoped he had just used a bad bag.

I finally gave it a slow turn before peering around, frantically searching for Donny. I was shaking when I stepped inside.

Everything was the same. You'd never believe that my brother went psycho just hours before. My work laptop and headset sat innocently on the kitchen table. Donny's things were in their usual pile next to the couch. I swallowed, hard, and forced myself to explore further. One cautious step at a time.

I couldn't get to my room because a pair of thin, hairy legs laid across the hallway and blocked my path. I gasped and shot to the bathroom, only to find my brother lying there, eyes open, no rise or fall to his chest, with a needle still in his arm. His phone laid cracked next to his hand. I scrambled to find a pulse only to recoil when his skin felt cold. The police would later rule it an overdose, but I knew he had killed himself. He couldn't live with what he had done to me or what he had welcomed into our lives. He didn't want to be a vessel.

I try to shake his limp, cold body out of my thoughts. He's not like that anymore. He's ashes now, and he's with me in Hollow Forest. I focus my efforts on hunting and gathering until it's too dark to see. Until I'm too tired to move anymore. Until my lids have to close.

I wake in the middle of the night to footfalls. Skeletor doesn't ruffle a feather and Laken remains asleep in her standing position. It's a few people and they're shouting.

"Chelsea, it's this way. It's the tree with the symbols," says a higher-pitched male voice.

I freeze. How do they know something like that?

"How do we get in again? What was it that Wyatt told us about?" another breathless male voice says.

"I can't believe he poofed into smoke," a woman's voice shrieks. Chelsea's, I assume.

If they keep this up, they'll lead the Canid straight to camp. I shuffle to my feet, Totto in hand, and bolt to the edge of the clearing, squinting through the fog. I knock three times on the tree, hoping they shut up and chill out before the Canid gets a whiff of their panic. The mist lifts in front of me like a curtain.

"I see someone in there. I thought I saw something move," Chelsea says.

"Me too," says the higher male voice.

"It's a trap, I bet," Chelsea says, a woman after my own heart.

"Well, it's our only shot," says the other guy, furiously tapping and knocking on the tree with the symbols.

He's doing it all wrong. He isn't knocking in threes, Wyatt isn't here to be the welcoming committee, and I'm left to try and usher them in here and calm them before the Canid catches up. I'm surprised it hasn't howled already. No whispers of my name.

"Three times. Oh my God," she screams, shoving him out of the way to start again.

I'm almost through to them. The fog is thin and there are only two pairs of trees left. But then the breathless guy has a motherfucking flashlight. He just flicks it right on. His face is lit up, and there are flashes of the others. Not much, but enough to know they are three tired, terrified, and desperate people.

"What are you doing, Dan?!" Chelsea screams. "You're going to—"

She shrieks as her arm is ripped off by a phantom, but no smell of wet fur smothers me. Blood spurts from her shoulder as she cries.

"Hold on," I yell.

I'm so close to them. I only have two more trees to knock on.

The one guy drops the flashlight while the higher-pitched man runs away, only to be tackled. Claw marks from something unseen shred his body. The torch gives a spotlight view of his death. Chelsea whimpers on the ground while she bleeds out. She's a foot away from me, afraid and in pain, as her blood creeps closer to my hiking boots. I stand, frozen, finally understanding.

The last guy left grows rigid. He slowly walks toward the phantom Canid, embracing his death, just like it wanted. The irony of the avoidance and then active participation in his own demise is like seasoning on the Fiend's meal. He's mauled, and the Canid Carey makes good on its promise. His death is quick.

All I want is to plunge Totto right into the Canid, end its tyranny on those who wander the Hollow. But the Canid isn't here. Their remains wear away, their body parts fade, an ear here, a foot there, demonstrating what scavengers did to their corpses over time. They shrivel and turn to soil, nothing but a pile of bones. And then they're gone, just like the blonde girl I first met. They are nightmares. Stains, as Wyatt called them, of gruesome death. I sheath Totto after staring at the spot where they dissolved into nothing.

# CHAPTER SEVENTEEN

DONNY'S FUNERAL WAS intimate. A few of his partier friends from my college collected in the back, murmuring to themselves, and shuffling their feet. I stood with my family in the very front pew. I couldn't help but look over my shoulder, over and over again, expecting Donny to say he was kidding. My joints felt stiff and rigid compared to the sloping doorways and stained glass of the church.

My mom sobbed quietly to herself with my dad's arm around her. My dad's other hand gripped my shoulder. The strength and resolve he showed now just made me angrier. Where was this support when Donny was alive? Was it all for show? He kept his gaze steadily on the ground. I fidgeted with my scarf, worried the long, thin bruises would peek out from the folds in the fabric. The church was decorated beautifully with purple ribbons for opioid awareness. The priest spoke of Donaldo Emanuel Soloman's willful spirit, even though Donny had never met him and stopped going to church long ago. His funeral wasn't standardized or cold like I thought it would be, though. The priest read Romans 8:38 and 39.

"'For I am convinced that neither death nor life, angels nor demons, neither the present nor the future, nor any powers, neither height nor depth, nor anything else in all creation, will be able to separate us from the love of God that is in Christ our Lord.'" The priest's voice rang through the church.

Goosebumps rose on my skin.

I waited while the guests had hugged, kissed, and choked out their "condolences" in my ear before they filed out of the church. I needed to have some alone time with my brother. When I got close to the urn with its gleaming silver surface and intricate designs, I could no longer hold back my hot, angry tears from spilling down my cheeks. Donny was continuously drowned in things that brought the worst out in him. Always restless. And what did he have to show for his life? Years of anguish, hiding, lies, and drugs? He was now only ashes and dust. My gaze followed the urn's spiraling pattern to the wide base. I clasped a hand over my mouth to stifle a scream. The urn rested carefully on that motherfucking book.

I used my anger to propel myself forward. I hugged the urn to my chest. While holding my brother, I ripped the book out from under him. There was no way I was going to have Donny be tortured by that Godforsaken thing. I set him back down carefully, and my tears dripped down the urn's sides. I shoved the book under my arm.

"I'll take care of this," I whispered, my face close. "I miss you, Donny. I hope you're alright now. I hope you're at peace."

I repositioned my scarf and made sure that the book was tightly tucked under my arm before making my way around the pews and out the door to spend time with my broken family.

My family never had a sense of cohesiveness. Its foundation was never smooth, which is why it shattered. So at camp, I create my own routine. I sharpen and polish Charm and City. I try to make more spears for Wyatt. They aren't as straight or sharp, but it helps me get used to using the different knives. I climb trees to strengthen myself and to look further into the wild woods. I hack off branches that reach into the camp with Totto and then hone in the end with Wyatt's knives. I can climb higher than I ever thought I could. I'll sometimes perch in the canopy and whittle while the trees hold me. It's during one of these searches for a tree to climb, that I find something.

One of the trees has a hole in it. It's practically dead with dried limbs and no leaves. The opening is about eye level and the size of a fist. It has smooth edges around the outside of its oval shape. There must have been a branch that fell off long ago. I should have noticed it sooner. There are layers of birch bark carefully piled on top of one another in a stack. I take them out slowly to examine them. On each curled square of bark is a brief, written message.

You are not alone

I will be back

Please rest and eat

Dont pet bird and treat horse nice

The next in the pile read:

This is a hidden place

Fiends in forest can't see

That isn't entirely true, though. I have to go in a certain way and knock and do a whole song and dance before I enter. The rest, well – I guess he got his point across. He's created a fortress and wants people to know that he'll return to help. He doesn't want people to be alone like him. Something's off about his constant hope. From what I saw of the Stains last night, he obviously worked with those people. He taught them where to run and hide. Why did they fail so miserably, and how does he help others when it's not entirely fool-proof here?

The rest of the stack has more information about things in the forest. Some I've met, like the Rot and Canid. Others he's talked about, like Stains and the Ruminant.

Ruminant
Old, original Fiend in the forest
Looks like a big deer
Four stomachs and antlers are pincers and four mouths
like wood chipper
Always hunts you—never tired—makes you crazy
Try to stab at neck under mouths
My skin prickles.

Stain
Someones soul is lost or eaten by Fiend
Places where they were most scared
Relives like recording
Death replays and replays
They stained the spot with their lifeblood forever

There was that girl with the braid. She was so scared when she realized she was alone and couldn't find her way out of the forest. She wanted so desperately to get out but didn't have the intuition to find the gate. Was she really just a recording? She felt so real. And those people who tried to get in last night? Are they nothing but a terrible memory set to replay again and again? Maybe Wyatt has to believe they're only a recording so he can live with what happened to them.

Army Bears
Have four front paws and two back
Four arms look like gorilla
Attack from above
Stab where head meets neck


Boar
Very small
Size of ladybug-looks like tiny boar.
Burrows into skin and eats organs

There is one that was tightly rolled into a cylinder that I almost lose as I shuffle through the different warnings and directions.

Chelsea
I wish I knew how to warn you
I wish I could hold you again
I came back and now your Stain haunts me

I swallow. There's a faded one that's brittle and has long since broken apart. When I piece it together, it reads:

Tyler Im so sorry
Your blood has stained the Forest
And your soul has stained my heart
I love you forever

Something tugs in my chest and tears prick my eyes. Is he talking about Chelsea? The one who got demolished last night? And who was Tyler? There's a cold knot in my stomach, but it isn't quite sadness. It's more fear of my own fate. Chelsea and

Tyler had the luxury of Wyatt. To know him. To be shown how to survive. To be loved by him. I have to swallow a lump in my throat.

I read through them all, sometimes multiple times. Some are clearer than others, but what I find to be evident, is Wyatt's need to see his encounters as helpful to someone else. If he records what he learns, then he has a purpose. He's there in someone's time of need.

The very last one in the pile drags a sob from my chest.

Am I even alive

Is this death

Is it worse than death

I get up, dust myself off, and carefully place them back in the tree's hollow. I feel like I've intruded, and at the same time, he's purposefully left them for someone to find. To believe he helps others. To have his calling when he is cursed to be in Hollow Forest forever. I turn back to the dome with a dead branch in one hand and Totto in the other. I'm going to whittle a spear, not touch the bird, and be nice to the horse.

# CHAPTER EIGHTEEN

I HAVE A lot of time to think while Wyatt's gone. It starts out with incessant worry loops. Who is Wyatt, really? How many people has he "helped"? Even if his heart's in the right place, is he really helping anyone? The last time I was forced to be this alone with my terrible thoughts was when I finally returned to my apartment after Donny died.

For a few days after Donny's funeral, I stayed with my parents. They were mostly silent and distant. When there was soft sniffling in the middle of the night and I found my mom kneeling and weeping quietly while surrounded by pictures of Donny at different stages of his life, I knew I had to leave. There was an actual argument over who would get Donny's ashes. I always thought I could just have them, but my dad was the one who put up the largest barrier.

"My boy belongs at home." My dad's words were thick with grief.

A laugh bubbled out of me. It was a hateful sound.

"Since when?" I spat. "I've been the one always there for him. He's always trusted me. I've never judged him."

"He stays here." My dad banged his fist on the countertop.

He raged and sneered at me while my angry tears plopped to the floor. It's one of the only times I recall standing up to him, but I'd be damned if Donny would be stuck here. We glared at each other.

"You say he belongs home, and that's never been here." I hated how shaky and scared my voice sounded.

Dad paled at the blatant disrespect. "My boy stays," he whispered before stalking out of the room. It was always worse when he grew quieter like that. I jumped when he slammed the door to his den.

My mom surprised me by gently placing my brother in my arms, not meeting my snarling face with her red-rimmed eyes.

"Hablare con papa, mija."

I nodded. "Gracias, mamita. Le extraño." I cried harder, my anger dissolved, revealing the giant monster that was my grief.

"Yo tambien." She sniffed and patted the urn in my arms.

It was on that day that I returned home.

My apartment felt like all the air had been sucked out of it. I got up, fought the urge to stay in my pajamas, changed into some business casual clothing, and continued to work every day. I put Donny's urn in the kitchen on its own end-table. I liked that he was there with me while I did my thing. He was out of the living room for a change.

I tried to navigate my life without taking care of anyone else other than myself. It felt strange, but they say taking care of yourself is what you should do before taking care of others. I always struggled with that, and look where my old ways had brought me.

I kept busy and I paid the rent early. I set up a food delivery service that put my groceries right outside my door and I actually spoke with my parents without having some kind of argument.

Or I guess they wouldn't call it that. They would say I was shutting them out. But responding to my dad's lecturing with comebacks in my head counted as a fight to me. My silence told them everything.

Some nights, there was a knock on my door and my brother softly said, "Angelita, are you up?" But it was only a dream. I avoided the bathroom as much as possible until the mirror inexplicably shattered and I had to sweep up the glimmering shards and my tears that littered the tiles. So much happened, but there was this internal pressure to keep going. Everyone told me that I should take time, that I needed to mourn the loss of my brother, that I needed to get out of my own space for a while. But I felt that I could just work my life around it. Sometimes I felt suffocated and left my apartment, but that was a good thing, wasn't it? Maybe I wouldn't be such a recluse.

Every once and awhile I'd wake up and wonder why Donny wasn't making eggs for us, or I'd text him to see if he wanted to order takeout, or I'd forward him a meme I thought would make him chuckle. Sometimes I forgot he was gone. I would do a walkthrough to pick up his piles of shit, and sob because my living room was completely clean.

My hurt was so deep that I was hollow inside. I'd cry myself completely out of tears or emotions. I was drained and it almost allowed me to ignore the signs that Donny was still with me.

Almost.

It started mostly in the bathroom, like with the shattering mirror, or finding some anti-panic pills on the floor. Other times his cracked phone, that I had long since stopped charging, would flash on with an outgoing call to the police. When I'd frantically try to hang up, it would go dark and cold in my hands. With time, the strange activity sprawled out to the rest of the apartment. Sometimes there would be wet spots on the couch, just like the ones that formed when I would catch him there crying and staring at pictures of Zach. Of course, I tried to ignore the weirdness. That didn't last long.

I made work my welcome distraction. I knew there would always be dissatisfied customers that called. I knew exactly what to say, and I knew how to fix it. If I didn't, it wasn't my problem, it was a transfer person's issue. So I plugged away at my quality assurance.

The headset helped me block out the occasional whispered apology that I thought I could hear. It was reminiscent of Donny's voice and echoed from the living room. It also helped me block out the shaking or dropping of pills in the bathroom. I didn't want to live with Donny's remorse or final days while I was trying to get my life back together. I learned that dwelling on the negative would only keep you from reaching your goals. You used your bad luck to double down and fuel you. That's exactly how I was able to graduate early after what Jacob did to me my freshman year, and that's how I was going to potentially get a raise or bonus with my job now. I could just ignore the moans and sobs and apologies that were probably just a result of my grief.

I was on a call with a lovely older woman who wanted to discuss her uneven cabinets. It was something I'd handled before. I'd make sure she felt heard. I'd make sure she felt like we could straighten something out in her life. It was 10 minutes and 22 seconds into the phone call when there was the zap click.

Fear prickled my forehead and back of my neck. Sweat poured and my eyes darted to the living room, looking for Donny. I tried to breathe through it. My vision tunneled and the old woman's voice became muffled. It took me back to the sage-burning, chanting, and my brother's unseeing eyes. I breathed in through my nose, out through my mouth, and clutched the kitchen table with both hands, squeezing my eyes shut.

"I'm sorry, ma'am." I tried to keep my voice even. "I can't understand you."

"You know what I don't understand?" My brother's familiar voice crackled on the other end like I was speaking to him on an old telephone. "Why I let my own fucking sister see me like this."

"What do you mean?" My whole body shook.

"They'll tell you I'm attached to you, but I'm trying to say I'm sorry."

"You've already said that. You can go now," I said through gritted teeth.

"I'm just . . . I don't know what to do."

"Go away. Find Zach or the right path or something. Find peace," I said. A cold knot formed in my stomach.

"I understand you being angry, I just—"

"No! No more, Donny. No more 'justs'. Because I could use justs too! I just found you dead. I just keep your fucking ashes in my kitchen. I just lost my big brother. I'm just all alone," I choked.

"I'm so sorry," his voice crackled.

"Stop apologizing. I'm sick of apologies. They're too late."

"I'm always too late, but she'll tell you that you aren't. But you can't help me. You have to stop trying to."

"What are you saying?"

"You know what I'm saying." His voice was soft, pleading. "You've done so much for me, and if there's a chance to avenge me, stop. I know I don't deserve it. And you definitely don't deserve it."

I wanted to hide away. This felt dangerous and unnatural.

"Please, Angelita." His scared voice broke me. "There's nothing, nothing you can do."

"There's nothing I can do?" I echoed. I fought against my heart, trying not to hope.

"I'm dead and have so many regrets. I should have protected you more," he said.

"Leave me alone!" I screeched.

"What do you mean there's nothing you can do?" the customer raged. "This is the absolute worst and most unprofessional service I've ever received, and you better be sure that you'll be getting a formal complaint."

She hung up the phone and I sat there with my headset on, my eyes still shut tight. I couldn't stop panting. I jolted up and practically threw my computer. I ran out of the apartment and hugged my knees to my chest on my welcome mat outside. It was later than I expected. I let the entire day flow past me. The thought that I had my chance to speak to my brother, that I could have said something soothing but instead chose to scream at him, made me cry into my hands. I knew I had to go for a walk. I bolted inside, grabbed my sunglasses and scarf, put my earbuds in, my Keds on, shoved down the panicked thoughts warning me of the terrors of the outside world, and marched out as if I had a purpose in life as if I knew where I was going.

The sea salt and din of a far-away crowd reminded me of happier times. I used the Ferris wheel as my North Star and felt my muscles relax when my foot first stepped onto the bustling boardwalk. I breathed in the salt air and let the currents of people wash around me like the ocean. Neon lights blinked, bright pinks and blues bathed people skipping, roller skating, and holding hands in that Ocean City glow. Donny and I used to sneak out of the house and lay on the cool beach at night. Or we'd hide out with vodka in water bottles, thinking we were so clever. As if our drunken laughter and staggering steps wouldn't be a dead giveaway. I stopped and let the crowds part around me. I stood still amongst the movement, hidden behind my nighttime shades and hood. I took out my earbuds and was swarmed by the crowd's chatter and the ocean waves' surge and slap at the sand. My eyes closed for a moment.

I felt a hand on my shoulder and gasped when I stared right into Donny's black eyes. He was forlorn and tried to talk, but no words came out.

"Donny," I said.

He turned away. I grabbed at him, but he was lost in the crowd. I shoved past people but I wasn't able to find my brother. The crushing weight of losing him all over again made me stumble out of the rushing crowd. I used the storefronts to support me. I felt a hand on my shoulder again, and I swiped at it. It was a thoughtless action, there was only fight in me. A fight to end my visions of my brother, a fight to end the sadness, a fight to stop tragedy.

"Whoa. I'm sorry. I just saw you, and—"

It was not Donny. It was a scared girl with a baby face, large blue eyes, and long, blonde hair. She couldn't be older than 15.

"What do you want?" I barked.

She held up her hands in an 'I surrender' stance. "I just—"

"Just, what?" My voice was cold and my heart was pounding.

"Never mind," she said, turning on her heels and flicking her blonde hair.

"No, wait." I wiped sweat from my forehead and tripped over people to keep up with her.

"I'm not supposed to do this kind of thing," she called over her shoulder. She stopped short in front of a neon sign that read

GASPARA'S SIGHT. It was a fortune teller's storefront. "But I see something, and it's big."

I laughed. It was a desperate laugh. "Okay, Gaspara. Are you going to tell me what's in my future?"

She put her hands on her hips. "Gaspara is my grandmother." Her face flushed. "And I wasn't going to rip you off like all tourists think Roma will do. I'm just trying to warn you."

"Warn me?" I thought of all the warnings I've had in the past. My parents, my priest, my friends, my supervisor. Did I ever listen? No. But maybe I should now.

"Yeah," she took a step forward. "Do you want to know?"

Did I?

I just stared at her.

"How about this," she said, facing away to find a solution to whatever the fuck this dilemma was. "I think you should at least have a name for what you're going through, and I don't fully know how to explain it myself. I'm still discovering my sight, but you're so clear right now. I can tell you at least a little bit about it. The rest of it, we'd have to ask my grandmother."

There was a hopefulness in her voice. She held a proud posture, one that said she knew what she was talking about and that her grandmother would know what to do with my life. Gaspara would have some way to fix it.

"Okay," I said weakly.

She folded her arms over her chest. "You have a spirit attached to you."

# CHAPTER NINETEEN

"When someone dies, their soul goes somewhere else. But you have an attachment. That means you're an anchor for someone's soul to keep them here on Earth, and the guy looks like you. He has your dark eyes and hair, so I'm guessing he's your brother." A little smile played on her lips when my jaw fell open, pleased she hit her mark. "He must have just died because he's the clearest spirit I've ever seen. Sometimes souls stay around for a little bit to say goodbye to their family, but you must be weighing him down."

"I'm weighing *him* down? You've got to be joking." The girl was startled when all the anger I've tried to hold in, finally flooded out. "The whole time, I was the only Goddamn person in his life holding him up. If anything, he held me back. I was always worried he'd bring home someone awful or I'd come home and find him—"

And that's when I burst into tears. Everything I feared had come true. He'd been abandoned. He felt like everything he did was wrong. He thought his love was dirty. I came into his life and made everything worse. It's like he tried to carve a space out in the world, but he never fit anywhere.

Tears and snot streamed down my face. People kept their distance from me as they passed. The girl's eyes were large and darting. She clearly didn't know what to do with a mess like me. She kept a solid distance between the both of us. An old woman with tanned skin and a weathered face peeked her head out of the open doorway to check on the commotion.

"Jessica," she hissed. The girl turned to the old woman. "What have you done to this poor girl?"

"Nonnina, I just—"

The old woman cut her off. "You just, what? Wanted to show off?"

The girl's face turned red and her eyes glistened with shame. "No, look," she said, pointing to the empty space next to me.

"I see," the old woman said and stepped out of her storefront. She reached out to me. I was grateful to have something to hold onto. Her gnarled hand was warm and soft in mine. "Follow me, dear. I know your loss has taken all of your strength. Please, come inside, just for a moment."

Their store was a bit tacky, with crystal balls, beads, stones, and those fucking bundles of sage all neatly stacked and placed. It was dimly lit and the air was hazy. Even though the woman gestured for me to sit at a table that was clearly visible to the passerby, it felt private and pleasant.

She sat down across from me and put both of my hands in hers, and without turning away from me, she said, "Jessica, come here. You started this, and you need to see it through." The young girl plopped next to me with a sigh. The woman gave my hands a squeeze. "I am Gaspara, and this is my granddaughter, Jessica." She gave me a smile and crow's feet creased at the corners of her eyes. "I apologize for her abruptness. These past few days have probably been very difficult," she said.

I nodded.

"With your permission, I can tell you what I see and maybe what I hear if I'm able to reach the soul that is attached to you."

Donny whispering against the wall flashed in my mind. He thought he was talking to Zach, and he'd been tricked. And here I was, staring into the concerned eyes of someone who said they could do the exact same thing. Something was alluring about having someone be able to talk to my brother. I needed to be careful.

I strained to hold Gaspara's gaze and nodded again.

"Okay," she said. And I thought she would close her eyes, but instead, Gaspara and Jessica both turned to a fourth chair that was at the round table. "Hello Donny, thank you for joining us."

My hair stood on end when Gaspara uttered his name out loud.

"He is very clear."

"Is that good?" I asked.

"I'm sorry, dear, but not really. Sometimes souls stick around for a couple days, but he's attached to you. That means—"

"I'm keeping him here, I know," I said sadly.

Jessica looked down.

"Not exactly. It's more like, he rooted himself to you so he wouldn't pass over."

"What?"

"He obviously cares about you a lot and wants to make sure he remains for some reason. He's very restless. I have a, um," she tapped her fingertips to her chest several times, "fluttering, in my chest when he tries to communicate."

"That definitely sounds like him. Everyone has been saying they hope he is at peace now, and I don't think I've ever known him to be at peace."

"That's going to make things difficult." Gaspara caught her breath. "He says to make sure you destroy the book." She looked at me, worried.

"I saw the book, too," Jessica piped up, trying to redeem herself. "Don't read it."

Gaspara raised a hand for Jessica to hush. "It doesn't seem like we have to tell you how dangerous that book is," Gaspara said quietly.

I shook my head. As soon as I brought the book home from his service, I practically threw it. I didn't want it touching me. It felt so strange and wrong tucked close to my body after Donny's funeral. I wanted it far away, yet at the same time, I had these thoughts that maybe I could figure out what Donny said or did. One time, I even thought about trying to talk to him if I would just look at the book. Maybe he read something wrong or dove in headfirst like he always did and hadn't taken the proper precautions. Those were fleeting ideas that were immediately washed away when I picture him strangling me, or his empty eyes when I found him dead in the bathroom.

"No, I know how evil it is."

"Good. Destroy it," she said. "Make it so that no one can use it."

"Understood," I said.

"No one must read it ever again."

I nod.

Gaspara and Jessica fell silent for a little bit.

"When I destroy the book, will that help Donny cross over, or whatever you said he needs to do? Like, not stay attached to me?"

"No dear, I don't think so. Your brother is a very tormented soul. He might stay earthbound forever," Gaspara said. Sadness oozed from her voice. It had a there's-nothing-we-can-do quality to it. I knew it well.

"Why would he do that? He has his boyfriend in Heaven, or wherever you go after. Couldn't he meet with him until he sees me later, like when I die?" I was asking Gaspara, but I was also turned to the empty chair, pleading with my brother.

"He says that it was his blind chase for Zach that made him put you in danger, and he can't forgive himself. He didn't mean for you to find him. He tried to call the police before he, oh no, I'm so sorry—before he killed himself?" Gaspara said.

Jessica looked to me as if to double-check if that was true.

"But now he can see Zach! It's what he wanted," I strained.

"Guilt, shame, and the need to protect you are keeping him here," Gaspara said.

"So my brother will just always be around? Stuck to me?"

A look passed between them. I didn't like it. It was mournful. "No. He will only be attached to you for a little bit," Gaspara said. "But he also is too distressed to cross over. He must have really gone too deep with evils he didn't understand."

"He's fucking stupid," I mutter. Flashes of his gleaming face as his hands closed around my throat made it difficult to fight back more tears. I pull my scarf higher on my neck.

"It feels like," Gaspara tilted her head to the side, her gaze far away. "He is fighting a timeline. It's like there's an event or anniversary that is coming up that will force him to detach from you. His shame will be too great, and if he isn't ready to cross over at that point, he will be caught in the rotation of the Earth, and never be given that chance again."

"I don't understand," I said, but I did. The anniversary of my rape was in a little more than a month.

He always said that he was never there for me, that he never should have left me alone at the party, that he never should have trusted Jacob. And it felt like the day he took me to the hospital so that they could do a rape kit, was the day he really believed what others said about him. That he was a low-life, loser, nothingness of a man. But that was the moment I felt safest. I hadn't wanted to tell my parents. I didn't want to go to the police. I just wanted to take the hottest shower ever, to boil my skin off, and start fresh. But Donny was there for every moment after.

She gave my hands another squeeze. "I'm so sorry, my dear. I wish I had happier news to tell you." She gazed into the distance again but then shook her head to bring herself back to the moment, back to me. "For now, just let your brother know how much you love him, miss him, and will remember him. I can tell how much you cared, and Donny is telling me how much you meant to him." She stood up, slowly.

"If I talk to him more, maybe make him feel loved and comfortable, could that help?"

She gave me a weak smile. "Maybe."

But she meant 'No'. Her voice was devoid of hope.

"What was the point of that?" I said, standing up quickly and almost knocking over the chair.

Gaspara struggled to stand and she tried to reach her hand out to me again. I couldn't be with those ladies anymore. I turned to go, to face the world. I should have known not to hold out hope for their kind of psychic shit they tried to sell. But I stopped and turned to them one last time.

"So that's it? You're just going to say you can help and then take one look at Donny and say he's just going to disappear?" It was darker and the neon lights glowed brightly, flashing pinks and blues across their faces. I couldn't see the ocean anymore, only hear it crashing.

They were just telling me my brother was a lost cause like everyone else in his life. They were just reminding me that everything I did wouldn't change his damaged trajectory. Futility at its best.

"You helped your brother on his journey through life more than you will ever realize," Gaspara said to my back as I stormed out of their shop.

Stepping back onto the boardwalk felt like I had entered a new world, one that was illuminated and fast compared to my grief. I was about to jump into the current of tourists, but someone called my name. It was Jessica. Her eyes glanced behind her, making sure Gaspara was not paying attention, before darting back to me.

"There's a way you can save your brother by using his essence. A way my grandmother didn't tell you," she said.

# CHAPTER TWENTY

FOR EVERY NIGHT that passes and Wyatt isn't back, a wall forms inside me. There are no more quick glances to the foggy tree line. I don't stay up and listen to the noises, hoping for soft footsteps, praying that it isn't a Fiend. No more ruminating on his notes left on parchment bark or questioning who Chelsea and Tyler are. No more silent tears and clinging to the urn to soothe my fears of not having the pull. Instead, I practice riding, gathering greens and blooms, hunting close by camp, collecting water, and creating somewhat of my own survival system. I finally gather enough courage to search for more supplies farther out. The Jackalope is putrid, and I need to haul more water.

I clamber onto Laken and have her walk around the edge of camp. I practice riding her a bit more, and perhaps I'm stalling. There are flashes of something along the outside border of the camp. It's a caramel and white goat head, searching and craning its neck, sniffing the air. Skeletor and Laken are unconcerned, even when I have to keep myself from yelping when there's another Rot. This one's a little girl, dressed in rags, emaciated. I'm almost sorry for her as her yellow eyes dart around, searching for something to consume.

She appears when her bare feet hit the red clay spots that sit along the border of camp. Wyatt's words ring in my mind: "They're shy. They're more afraid of you than you are of them." I clap my hands together. It just scares Laken and makes her jolt to the side, almost throwing me off. I steady myself and try to hiss, but I'm too quiet. The Rot cranes her neck to peer through the fog. I don't want her to know where the camp is. We've worked too hard to be found out now.

I withdraw Totto and click my tongue. Laken picks up the pace to a trot. I make sure my Owletta mask sits securely and that I drape the feather hide on my shoulders just like Wyatt did with his Ruminant skin. We navigate the zig-zag pattern to leave camp and emerge from the fog. The Rot girl faces us and bleats. Her tongue sticks out as she throws her head back. There's a rumble in my throat, a growl. I screech with my own feral noise. Her eyes roll and she darts away.

I give a sigh of relief, relax my muscles, and loosen my hold on Totto. I need to make sure I don't get lost again like last time. I pass by the first tree, lean over, and hack at the trunk with the machete. The goal is to make a mark in the tree, just a little notch, to keep track of where we're going. All I do is spook Laken.

When I squeeze my legs and reach, the constriction makes her bolt forward. I accidentally fling Totto, the shining silver metal disappearing in the low ferns. My face is tight and I focus to keep my breathing even as that wet fur smell hits my nose. It's the Canid Carey again.

The reins are gripped tightly in my fists and I focus on how the crudely cut leather rubs roughly in my flesh. I just need to get off, grab the knife, and get back on. I'm not letting the Canid pull at my fears. I dismount and clutch at the machete. My palms are so sweaty that it slips through my hands.

I snatch up Totto and struggle to put it in the sheath at my hip. I just need to climb back on Laken. It's simple. I've practiced getting on and off at camp. Laken snorts and trembles.

"Angela," it whispers. It's like the faint rustling of leaves and wind. It's the decaying connection from an ancient creature.

It's practically breathing down my neck, an invisible demon on my back, waiting for me to fail, encouraging me to accept death. I close my eyes for a second and place my palms on Laken's skin. Her muscles quiver. She wants to run, but she forces herself to stay. Laken is steadfast in the Hollow Forest she calls home. She's survived thus far, and so can I. The Canid won't overcome me.

I breathe, feel Laken's warm skin, twirl my fingers through her coarse hair, and leap onto her back. She shoots forward before I swing my right leg completely over. My fists are tight on her mane and reins as I scramble the rest of the way on her back. Pounding footfalls of our predator thunder parallel to us. Occasionally there's a flash of dark red or rusty brown. Just a glimpse. Is it the Canid Carey, or dead leaves fluttering to the ground?

"Easy, girl," I say while gently leaning back in my seat, not wanting to get too far from camp without memorizing my bearings. I put that not-so-successful notch in the tree behind me, but nothing since. The Canid plods over to us. It howls, shrill then low, baiting me, boring its terrible call into my core. My bones rattle.

My eyes flash to someone to my right. Jacob's entitled chuckle is soft and I can't tell if it's in the back of my mind or coming from somewhere deeper in the forest. He isn't really here. He can't be.

Laken pauses, frozen in place. She bares her sharp teeth and lays her ears back.

"We are hunting," I whisper. "We are minding our own business and hunting. Ignore it. It can't hurt you or me. Just ignore it." My voice wavers and my mouth is dry. All I need is something to drink.

I force Laken to walk at a gradual pace. I breathe in after all four of her hooves hit the ground, and then out again as she walks four more steps. In. Two. Three. Four. Out. Two. Three. Four. The white, feathered Owletta pelt flutters and I pretend I'm a Fiend of the forest. When my muscles relax, so do Laken's. She looks to me for direction, and I want to make us okay. If Jessica and Wyatt are right, it can't latch onto our scent, or "aura," if I keep myself calm. I need to blend into the forest so the Canid won't prey on my lifeblood. For all it knows, I'm an Owletta.

I face trees ahead of me, refusing to check over my shoulder. There are three magpies, chirping and cooing. Their azure wings and black beaks are stunning. But I'm hungry and desperate. Their blood would quench my thirst. Their meat was probably delicate and dark. The Canid's mind warp pressures my skull. I get tunnel vision, smell copper, and dream of drinking the juices of the magpies. I want to go back and meet the Canid. To smile at it with red-stained teeth.

I want to run to it. I want to face it and dive into its abyss, to get it over with. It will help me breathe and live forever. I don't want to live in fear anymore.

I shove the thoughts aside. I freeze, wink one eye, whisper Charm's name, and throw the knife at the magpies, setting out after my goal of hunting by horseback. I'm not letting the monster deter me. I'm liberated as the knife flies through the air.

I miss them by a long shot. It arches feet below the branch, and the three magpies fly away in a flurry. I focus on the next task, leading Laken over to the fallen knife.

I shake my head, trying to clear it. In. Two. Three. Four. Out. Two. Three. Four. It's trying to trick me into welcoming it, into letting it alter my path, into seducing me into its forgotten death. I don't want to be just another Stain on this land. I don't want to mar the earth with my lifeblood. The Canid Carey already has enough. It's drunk with fear and doubt and pain, and its greed is showing.

I slip off her back again and snatch up Charm. There's a battle of thoughts in my mind. Laken snorts and tosses her head. The reins bite into my hands and I almost lose them. I hold tighter. I can't let her go. I bend down to reach Charm. It's vulnerable in a squat position next to a powerful kelpie. She whips her head up to yank the reins from my grip and almost pulls me over. I stand up and jerk the reins down like Wyatt does when she defies him.

Laken rears back, pulling me almost under her. She kicks at me with her front hooves.

I jump back, yanking the reins again. Why is she pawing at me? We've worked so well together. Can the Canid control her?

"Laken, no," I say.

She clambers to her front hooves with flattened ears and her sharp teeth bared.

"Don't you show your teeth at me," I growl at her. "You don't treat Wyatt like this, and I'm not going to let you walk all over me. Not with the Canid around. We're a team. We have to be a team."

She tries to spin in a circle in an attempt to kick at me. I root myself to the spot and she ends up lunging around me for a moment. She huffs and snorts, but then stops and walks toward me.

"Easy, girl. See, we're in this together."

She comes so close with sorry, milky eyes. She puts her

muzzle down to breathe on my face. I reach my hand and pet her cheek, accepting her apology. She jerks her head to the side as if she's alerted to something in the woods. I look with her in that direction, too. I squint to see what she sees.

While I'm distracted, she slams her head into the front of my face and it throws me to the ground. Black spots blot my vision and I let go of her in my fall. Laken takes off into the woods, kicking leaves and sticks into my face.

My lip is hot and pulses while my front teeth feel loose and sore. I touch my front tooth with my tongue and it wiggles a bit. I try to stand up and am dizzy. I'm worried I'll get attacked while I'm vulnerable, but the Canid's scent and the pressure on my mind is lessening. I spit, expecting a tooth to come out, but there's just pink saliva.

I lean against a tree. Laken screams and bolts further into the woods. She approaches a short silhouette that's running in our direction. What is it? Was she protecting me like she did with the rabbit? She charges and leaps, dancing around it.

I pick up Charm, my head pounding. The figure waves its limbs in the air. I'm not leaving her to fight alone. I run on foot, my feathered hide flaps behind me, the skull bounces a little on my head. I have much better footing than when I first entered Hollow Forest. I leap over sticks and avoid muddy patches where I would have slogged through and tripped over before. I'm supposed to be here, meant to be here.

Laken huffs and snorts to ward off the predator. I hide behind a tree, catch my breath, and clutch Charm tighter. I'll throw it, hopefully with better accuracy than the magpies, and hack at them with Totto when I get closer. I dodge to another tree, staying out of sight. I'm silent. As soon as Laken moves out of the way, I'll exhale and throw as hard as I can. She's still blocking the shadow from me as she huffs and prances.

I breathe in.

Hold it.

Breathe out.

Throw.

Only to realize it's Wyatt standing there naked while Laken loses her mind at their reunion. I scream, the only way to articulate a warning.

Charm flies, handle over point over and over again. It's quick and accurate. He turns, surprised by the scream. I just got him back. How can I make him disappear again?

"Charm, stop," he says, throwing his hands up.

Charm stops mid-air, inches from his throat, and drops to the ground. I have to lean against the tree I was hiding behind to steady myself. My legs wobble, threatening to give out. He bends down and grabs Charm.

"Shit, Angela. You trying to knife me again?" My heart stops until a big, broad smile spreads across his face.

I blink away tears and sprint to him. Before I can think about it, we embrace. Relief rushes through me. He hugs me back, tightly. My security. All the loneliness melts. The words that helped me hunt and navigate through the forest while he was gone race through my head. Our hearts pounding together rhythmically. He's warm and solid in such a cold world. I finally pull away a bit. His nose and my beak inches from each other. His sable eyes crinkle at the corners.

"I'm really happy to see you and so glad you're still here, especially after, how many nights?"

"Sixteen," I say.

"Whoa. I never usually know how long I'm gone." He winces

at his own words, and lets go of me. We both know what he means. He'd prepared himself to meet my Stain when he came back, just like many others. Just like Tyler.

"But um, anyway, I am feeling a little exposed. Would you mind?" He reaches out a hand.

"Right, sorry." My cheeks grow warm and I'm again thankful for the Owletta skull obscuring my face. I fumble with the leather straps that secure the hide over my shoulders. I give it to him and he tucks it around his waist like a towel, exactly like how I first met him.

"That's better," he says, smiling. I can't meet his gaze. "Let's get back to camp." He clears his throat.

I nod and hop on Laken's back.

"Wow! You've definitely been practicing. Look at you!"

My face warms again. "Sorry, did you want to get on first?"

"No," he says. "You're all good." He swings on her back and the heat of his skin radiates from him. It's strange being around someone else after so long by myself, even if he might not be alive, even if he's a ghost.

"Ready?" he asks, reaching around me and holding onto Laken's mane.

"Yep," I say, swinging Laken around and clicking my tongue, ready to show off.

We race through the woods. Laken's feet pounding and scattering leaves behind us. The air we cut through flings my jagged hair inevitably into Wyatt's face. The smell of earth fills me up as we race to our home.

# CHAPTER TWENTY-ONE

"WE'RE OUT OF water, huh?" said Wyatt. Skeletor bounces at his feet. Ever since we came back, the bird won't leave Wyatt alone. I boil with jealousy when Skeletor left me for days at a time, but for Wyatt, he'll peacock around, flaunt his feathers, and lovingly rub his head against Wyatt's freckled cheeks.

"Yeah," I say, taking off the Owletta skull.

"How have you made it this far with no water?" he asks, scratching Skeletor between his wings.

"I found a little spring. And when we killed stuff, I think the blood helped Laken. Skeletor seems to be okay."

"Yeah, Skeletor takes care of himself," he said, a worried smile spreads across his face. His eyebrows furrow. "Listen, we definitely need to go on a water run," he says. "I know we just got back, but we need it now. You look too skinny, dehydrated, and tired."

"Gee, thanks," I say. Why was he so worried?

"Well, there are several places, but the closest place would be the river," he says.

My heart pounds.

"Where the berries are?" I ask.

"Yes. But we don't have to stay long. We will run there, bring the water skins, and come right back, but I can tell that you and Laken are dehydrated." He walks into the dome to get the water skins. When he comes back out with them he says, "and I also think that even though you have some not-so-good experiences there, that you clearly have learned a lot. I'll be right there with you. You've grown so much, and that river is not going to get the best of you. We'll do it together."

"Okay," I say again, about to put the skull back on.

"Hold up," Wyatt says. "We have to take care of that hair of yours."

"What do you mean?" I ask, trying to hold back a smile.

Wyatt's eyes dart around, trying to come up with the best wording to break it to me how shitty my hair is. "It's just that when we ride, it sometimes, flies around."

"Uh-huh, and what if I used one of those leather strap things to tie my hair back like you use with your dreads?" I try to keep my face straight.

"You could, you could," he says, nodding his head and looking at his hands. "It's also a little bit uneven."

"But I cut it myself."

"Yeah, and I'm sure it helped. I could even it out in the back if you'd like."

"I kind of like it like this." I run my hands through my matted, jagged strands.

"Okay," he said "that's totally fine. Thought I'd offer."

His face is distraught. That's when I can't contain myself any longer. I laugh.

"Oh my gosh, Angela. You were joking?"

"Yeah. I know it's a rat's nest, Wyatt. Please help me cut it."

I sit down in front of him while he kneels behind me. Goosebumps rise as his rough hands brush against the back of my neck and he gathers my hair into one twisted rope. I try my best to keep my head straight and my neck firm as he cuts into it, though it feels more like sawing, each strand snapping as they're sliced. He isn't Jacob. He's gentler. He's kinder. He's Wyatt.

"There." He leans forward and shows the wad of hair to me.

I run a hand down the back of my greasy head. The ends just barely graze my collar bone. I'm lighter.

"Thank you," I say, still pulling on the ends. "I've never had it this short before."

"Do you like it?"

"I don't know, yet. I think so? It's definitely better than that nest you're holding in your fist," I say, embarrassed when he's still gripping the wad of spiky ends.

"You look great," he says.

"Thanks." I can't look right at him. "Do I need to bring my backpack?"

"No, I usually tie the water skins loosely around Laken's neck. You could bring your empty skins and gallon jug, though. We can tie them all together."

"Sounds good," I say and help him drape the skins over Laken.

He's right. You could tell she's dehydrated. She hangs her head low, defeated. Her milky eyes are bloodshot and her skin is wrinkled and flakey. I'm such a failure. She's a water creature. She was literally found in a lake, named after it. Maybe she needs to submerge in water every now and again.

"Alright, let's go," Wyatt said.

We both mount Laken and it's a much faster trek on horseback than it was when we snuck away on foot carrying the dead Owletta. There's a soft glow as the sun sets. Skeletor's faint silhouette sweeps above. The branches shake and flutter as I sway on Laken below. I smell the crisp water before we get to it. The river is beautiful in the fading light and the berries appear just as delectable as before. But I know what they'll do to a person. I shove the images of Jacob's glistening, predatory eyes away and listen to the peaceful sound of water over river rocks.

"You okay?" Wyatt asks.

"Yeah. Just glad it's not too far from camp," I say.

"Agreed," he says as we both dismount.

Laken bounces and shakes her head. Her mane is bewitching and wild as it whips. Wyatt holds her steady while I untie the water skins. He takes off her makeshift bridle and she bolts into the water. She paws, splashes, and screams with joy. Wyatt puts his hands on his hips and laughs out loud as she sinks below the surface and throws her head to fling water at us. Large gills slit both sides of her neck as she plunges into the water again and again.

He takes off his Ruminant skull and hangs it on a lower branch.

"This is usually where I reappear," he says. "My mouth is almost always dry and I wonder if it's like my body knows I need water, so I come here. Even if I've been fooled by those venom berries a time or three before."

"Three times?" I ask. I like watching him lovingly stare at Laken while he crouches at the water's edge. His beautiful smile lights up his face and his eyes sparkle with familiarity and pride.

"Oh yeah," he says, dipping the skin below the water's surface. "The first time, I was desperately hungry. The second time was to try and figure out what I had seen the last time. And the third one was to see if I was even alive."

Images of Donny's bloodshot eyes and yellow foamed mouth flash in my mind.

"You tried to kill yourself?" I swallow and join him on the bank.

"I felt really alone here," he says. "It was more of an experiment with nothing to lose."

"Yeah, well, that sounds like trying to kill yourself to me."

I'm heartbroken and furious at how casually he mentions it. How could he think it was okay to "experiment" like that? Suicide is such a permanent decision. The trauma ripples out and affects everyone. My breath is rapid and shaky. We're both silent as we filled the rest of the skins.

"What did you see?" My throat is tight.

"Honestly, it doesn't make any sense. It wasn't as concrete as what you probably saw."

I flinch when I remember being frozen and Jacob over me.

"It was more of a feeling. Like, my fear was feeling alone in this white, cold room. Sometimes I think that's where I go when I disappear."

"Like, Heaven?"

"I hope that's not what Heaven is like. Unless I'm dead and that's what the afterlife is? But it felt more solitary and lonely than anything I've ever felt. Maybe that's why sometimes I get that intuition to be different places at different times, to try and help people as best I can."

"Maybe you're stuck in-between, like my br—like why I'm here now. I'm trying to help someone stuck in-between. That's what this one fortune teller girl told me. And what I know is that you're definitely not alone. You're helping me. And you have Laken and Skeletor, too."

"Well, it's my fear I guess, so I know how to avoid it. Even if I just help one person." He smiles at me. "And now I know that death by Owletta is slow and painful."

I was drained when the Owletta attacked me. A sense of pride and vengeance rises in me as I straighten the skull mask and pull the hide tighter around my body.

"I hope Totto didn't hurt you. I didn't mean to stab you. I'm so sorry," I whisper.

"Well, it definitely wasn't fun, but it was one of the quicker deaths I've had here. I'd rather disappear than become a Stain."

Tension grows. I could become one. We're dragged from imagining that possibility when Laken plods onto the bank and shakes. Water droplets sprinkle us.

"Laken, geeze," Wyatt laughs.

As the cold water droplets hit me, I realize it's been a while since I've bathed. How long has it been? I'm filthy. The dirt and oil are like an extra layer on my skin.

I clear my throat.

"Um, Wyatt?" Shame oozes from my voice. "Would you mind, um, standing watch while I rinse off in the stream?"

"Oh, yeah, sure. Man, I've been a bad host. I didn't even think to offer. I even have this, like, porous rock I bring with me to bathe. There isn't really any soap here, but there are these roots close to where I found Laken and it cleans you right up. Maybe we can get some tomorrow," he says quickly.

"Just, um, just turn around and don't look, okay?"

"I definitely won't," he says, already facing the other direction.

"Okay, one second," I say, trying my best to take off the layers as quickly as possible. I push away the vision of being naked and vulnerable here before.

I'm all bare skin and goosebumps as I run into the water. A squeal escapes my lips.

"What's wrong?" Wyatt's voice is filled with concern but he still doesn't turn around.

"Nothing, sorry. It's just absolutely freezing cold in here," I say, forcing myself into the water.

My breath catches in my throat as the icy water closes over my head. I open my eyes a little. The water is clearer than I thought it would be. I run my fingers through my short hair and massage my scalp. I wish I had shampoo and conditioner. I shiver when I break through the water again. The dirt gives way to clean, new flesh underneath. The filth washes down the river, quickly diluting in the water. I rub at my arms and shoulders. They're tighter and I have muscle definition. My limbs are different. My softer thighs have given way to powerful legs. My toes wiggle over the slimy river rocks making them send clattering vibrations. When I wash as much as I can in the freezing current, I rush out. I shake my head and my short hair slaps against my face.

"You done already?" Wyatt asks.

"Yes, but don't turn around yet," I say, trying to snake my way back into my gear. Dirty clothes stick to my wet body.

"I won't. Just checking," he says.

"Okay." I grab the feathered hide and mask in my arms.

He turns around and smiles. "Feel better?"

"Much," I say, shivering.

"You were so quick. I wonder if you wouldn't mind if I took a dip? After I come back, my skin is absolutely crawling. Cold water helps."

My pulse thuds in my neck. It gets dark here quickly. "No. I don't mind," I say.

"I'll be really fast." He throws off his clothes as he runs toward the water.

I turn away. I focus on Laken who lays down on the

embankment and rolls, getting mud all over her refreshed, pink skin. So much for her bath.

"Laken is rolling," I shout.

"Yeah, she always does that," he says.

He splashes into the water and sucks in a deep breath when the coldness hits him.

"I appreciate you turning around," he calls back, "but you've already seen it all. I don't really care."

"I'll give you your privacy," I respond.

But there's a warmth in the pit of my gut. I'm dizzy. There's a giggle stuck in my throat and I press a hand to my mouth so it doesn't escape. He said he didn't care, so I take a quick peek behind me.

The water comes up to his mid-waist. His broad shoulders shimmy in the water as he cleans his feet and rubs his legs. Luckily his back is to me. I grow hot despite the cold water still dripping off me. I snap back the other direction. What the Hell? Why wouldn't I give him his privacy? I'm hot and my skin prickles, feverish. I hear him move and splash, hastily rubbing the ice-cold water all over himself, trying to get rid of his pins and needles. I need to be more proactive instead of just listening to him bathe like a weirdo.

I put the Owletta skull and hide back on, already more protected. I need to finish filling the water skins he hung up on the same low-hanging branch by his Ruminant mask. I keep my gaze down to avoid looking at him while I collect the supplies. There's a part of me that wants to look again, that's curious. His skin is so smooth, his smile enchanting. My stomach does a flip when I imagine how close he'll be to me on our ride home. But I push the thoughts away. I don't understand what's going on with me.

His skull, hide, and water skins are laced like a large charm bracelet on the tree branch. My eyes dart to the skull. It's wobbling. Two little hands grip it.

"Wait," I whisper, reaching out to grab the skull. I smack at the hands and rip the mask out of their sneaky grip. The little fists belong to a kid.

It's a small boy with brown hair and large, blue eyes. He has dirt on his chubby cheeks and he glares at me, despite my mask.

"Give it back," he says. "It'll help me hide."

Is this little boy a Stain? All of those missing kids who are never found. What if they've wandered into Hollow Forest? All those grieving families, wondering where they are. I can't watch this boy turn to dirt like all the others have. I don't want to watch his death.

I clutch the Ruminant skull to my chest, shut my eyes, and shake my head.

"Look, you can eat that man, there," the boy points to the direction of the river.

Wyatt makes quick splashes as he gets out of the river. I force my eyes not to linger on his waist, then his hips, then lower. I'm being such a creep.

"We need the mask. It helps us hide when we're hunting. You don't need it. You've planted your berries."

The boy smiles. His lips stretch a bit too wide.

We? What does he mean, *we?* As if to answer my question, two other kids come out from behind trees. An androgynous one has long, stringy, blond hair, and is about ten. The other little one is maybe eight or nine, around the same age as the chunky boy talking to me. He takes a step forward, pointing at the Ruminant skull in my hand.

"No," I say. "Go away."

My hand darts to Totto at my side. Am I really going to draw a weapon on a couple of kids?

Skeletor makes a long, piercing call from above and my hair stands on end. He's silent in his flight, but I feel better that he's somewhere near.

"Oh, you're sneaking too," says the brown-haired boy with a wide smile.

His pupils dilate to the size of quarters. They recognize me for the weak human I am.

"Very clever." His lips curl back to reveal rows of little, pointed teeth.

He opens his disgusting mouth. His jaw unhinges, like a snake about to swallow its prey. I take quick steps backward and hold Totto out, threatening them. The other two kids smile with their sharp teeth and run toward me. Their steps are too short and quick to be human. I'm about to hack at the boy with Totto when one of Wyatt's black knives plunges into his little chest. His wide, dilated eyes stare at the black blood pouring from the wound as he pulls it from his body. The two other kids click their jaws black into place. They make a scratchy whine and hover over their felled brother. Wyatt grabs my arm and we awkwardly race to Laken. It's difficult to have sure footing with the Ruminant ensemble and Totto still clutched tightly in my arms.

He fumbles with the mask and cloak while I put the bridle on Laken. We both wordlessly mount her. Laken snorts and her ears are flat against her neck as she gallops into the darkening woods. We both keep our blades in hand as Laken runs the direct path home. It doesn't take long for the two kids to catch up. They run on all fours, their thin limbs as nimble as a deer's. Their joints jut and angle like a spider's. They are wild things, hungry for us.

One runs alongside and leaps at us. Laken tries to kick it, but it jumps out of the way almost mid-air. Laken's ears turn and search for their practically silent footfalls. Totto and I hack at the long-haired one when it lunges. It howls as it collapses. Its ear hangs by just a bit of skin on the side of its head. I can tell we're getting close. I don't want them to know where the camp is. Wyatt swipes at the last one that's still chasing us and misses. It hops to the side too quickly, easily keeping pace with Laken.

"What the fuck are these things?!" I yell as it jumps at us again, jaw unhinged, wanting to swallow us whole.

"Hold on," Wyatt says.

He keeps a grip on Laken's mane and swings his body low. He practically sits on the side of her as we barrel closer and closer to camp. The fog is thick ahead. We're almost safe.

Wyatt swings his arm out like he was throwing a Frisbee, and his black knife slices into the thing's arm. It clicks its teeth together, gnashing them in pain, and thrashes on the ground. We run right to the symboled trees, knocking hastily three times. Laken snakes between each one. We are seconds from our oasis. It isn't until we made it to the clearing that Laken stops so abruptly that I slide up her neck, my mask clanging on my head.

Wyatt jumps off and practically throws his mask on the ground. He offers to help me dismount Laken. I wave him away and slip off of her neck, leaning on her for support. My legs and arms quiver with adrenaline. Laken's chest rises and falls heavily, her sightless eyes darting and her ears twirl and rotate. She tries to pick up on any giveaway to impending danger.

"I think we lost them," Wyatt says. "Even if they did try to follow us in here, they'd get scorched."

"Again, what the fuck were those things?" I say. I'm screaming the question. I have no control over my voice.

"Shh, Angela, we need to stay a bit quieter around those.

They're good at hunting. They're smart like the Canid. I don't know exactly what they are. I've only seen them once or twice before, but I call them split-faced kids."

"Children. I hacked off a child's ear."

"You and I both know that they are not actual kids. Okay? They really aren't. I've seen one shimmy up a tree and eat a whole bird, and I mean literally whole. Just swallowed it up while it squawked." He grabs my shoulders and faces me to him. "Look at me, Angela. Don't let them trick you. They're smart little shits. You did great out there. You handled Laken like a pro. You were absolutely fearless. No wonder you're still around." Words are flying out of his mouth so quickly. I don't like that he's rattled. I don't like him scared.

"Can you stop fucking saying that? How am I supposed to not let fear get to me when you keep talking about Stains all the time?" I'm shouting again.

"I'm sorry. I'm so sorry," he says. "Here." He yanks a water skin from the rope and shoves it at me. "Drink."

I like having something to do. The water skin squishes in my hands and I touch it to my lips. It stayed cold and is a welcome sensation to keep me grounded. I'm still alive. Wyatt is still here. We are both whole and okay. We sip and finish most of a pouch each before either of us speak again.

He takes his time petting and whispering to Laken to soothe her. Laken's agitated stomps and swishing tail slow. Her filmy eyes no longer roll and her ears don't flick. Wyatt grabs what looks like a bladder of something. He dabs red juice on her legs. The brambles and sticks must have cut her. She paws in protest but gives in to his treatment.

"It's acid from a root," he says. His voice makes me jump. "It helps her heal." He continues to rub the fluid in her cuts.

Laken's skin quivers while he generously applies the red substance.

"We're both tired," he says when he's finally finished. "How about you take the moss bed and I'll sleep with Laken. She's pretty shaken up."

"No, no. You just got back," I say, motioning for him to follow me into the dome. "And I added more moss and leaves and stuff."

"Whoa, you certainly did." He eyes up the bed. "It's like, double what it used to be, and are these more spears?" He admires the whittling I've done while he was away. "This is fantastic. I could teach you how to fish at the lake, and Laken deserves to have a treat." He looks at me, really looks at me. "You've definitely thrived."

I can't help but be proud.

"And I'm sorry if I ever made you feel like you wouldn't make it. That's exactly the opposite of what I want to have happen. I'm really just trying to help as best I can. It's the only time I feel the intuition or what you call 'the pull'. I'm just relieved."

"Me too."

I've been so scared and lost. I only have a week left before Donny is stuck here forever. I miss that pull and worried about Wyatt. We're both standing so close.

He gives a little smile. "Okay, I'm going to get Laken settled," he says, rubbing his arm.

"I wouldn't," I say, my voice breaking a little. I clear my throat. "I wouldn't mind if you stayed in here."

"No, no really. I'll be right outside," he says.

"Well, we could switch. You could have the bed, and I could be out by Laken." What the heck am I saying? Those creepy split-faced kids could be running around out there and waiting to find the secret way in.

"No, you should have the bed."

"I would like it, if you stayed." I swallow. "I would feel safe, if you stayed," I take a step back, "with me."

"Oh." Wyatt is hesitant. "Sure. Right." He takes off the hide and folds it.

I forgot I'm still wearing my gear. Here I am, a weird bird lady, asking a man to stay with me. Ridiculous. I take off my pelt and skull mask, too. We both go into the dome.

"Thanks." I crawl onto the moss and leaves.

"Yeah, of course. Those are some nasty Fiends out there," he says, trying to keep a healthy distance on the bed between us.

I roll away from him, the heat from Wyatt's body on my back. We aren't touching, but it's the closest I've ever been to someone. There are woven branches, trees, and fog in front of me, my fighting partner behind me, and I can't recall a time where I felt safer.

# CHAPTER TWENTY-TWO

I WAKE UP earlier than I expect, yet I'm rested. I roll over to Wyatt next to me. He's sleeping on his stomach. He looks so carefree with his locks laying every which way and his breaths slowly coming in and out. I count them as his back rises and falls. There's no way he's a ghost. He's too real, too alive, and too human.

It's a long time before I get up and tiptoe around him. Laken gives a little snort at me when I come out of the dome. I unlace a water skin and she drinks her fill. Her muzzle just barely fits inside and she guzzles the entire gallon. Her neck ripples as she quenches her morning thirst. She touches her dripping muzzle to my cheek. My mind shoots back to yesterday when she head-butted me. But this time, she's actually thanking me. I scratch her forehead before going back to the dome.

"You're up early," Wyatt says in a groggy voice as I open the leather flap.

I smile at him as he sits upon the bed of moss and rubs his eyes.

"Yeah, I slept well." I can't remember the last time I've been able to say those words.

We silently collect ourselves. Does reappearing exhaust him?

Does he have to physically work to pull himself together? It must be an awful thing, to not be solid.

"You ready? I want to show you some good things about the forest. I feel like you haven't had a proper tour."

My heart pounds, but I'm a little curious at the same time. I don't say anything.

"Come on. Laken needs it, and I think you need it." He smiles and nudges me to be more comfortable. "It's morning time. Most of the Fiends will be asleep."

"Ha! Most?" My chest tightens and only lets little breaths in and out.

"Come on. It's better to just do it and not think about it too much."

"What about those things? The kids with the teeth?"

"They're long gone by now, I'd expect. Laken would be letting us know, and I'll double-check with Skeletor if that'll make you feel better."

He whistles three sharp notes and waits with his head to the side before I respond.

"Come on, we might need to be outside. He's probably hunting."

I hope my slight twinge of apprehension isn't going to attract the Canid. Even if I'm a bit uneasy about being out in the forest, it's not like I feel the pull anyway. I haven't felt it for a while now. And with my traumaversary just a few days away, I need to try anything and everything to get it back.

We dress in our gear and walk out of the dome with spears, rope, and Laken in hand. He makes three short whistles again, looking up at the clearing in the canopy. Skeletor sails into view. He circles and glides high above the trees.

"How would he be able to see?" I ask.

"He just does," Wyatt says. "Trust me. He's scouting."

He gives three short whistles one last time before Skeletor gives three screeches back.

Wyatt looks satisfied. "We're all good."

"What? How do you know? What does he do when it isn't good?"

"He'll make one, long cry. It'll sound like a warning."

Every noise Skeletor makes sounded horrifying to me, but I'm not going to argue with Wyatt. If he says everything is alright, then I believe it. He knows how to navigate the forest well-enough, even if he's died more than a few times before. We both mount Laken, and before long, we're on our way.

Laken keeps a steady pace while Skeletor flies high overhead. I sometimes catch a glimpse of his rusty feathers sailing above the dense canopy. We pass rows of trees, scratchy bark, and pine needles.

Three long scratches are cut into some of the trunks. Bark is ripped away in jagged claw marks. They aren't deep, but they are substantial enough to cause some sap to ooze. There's something intimate, menacing. It's a mark, a warning, and a way to keep score. My hand lurches to my side.

I'm reminded of that damn blue book. After I got the directions from Jessica, I practically ran from her back to my place. I clutched the papers with scrawled directions in my sweaty hands as I entered my apartment.

My mind was reeling from what Jessica told me. My notes didn't make any sense at all. Halfway through the "rules" she discussed, I decided I wasn't going to do it. Besides, a part of me still thought I might be just another sucker in a fortune-telling scam. Who knew? Maybe they were the ones who sold Donny all of his séance shit. I wasn't going to be made the fool. And it would start with destroying that fucking book.

I pulled the tome from the junk drawer and threw it onto the kitchen table. It slapped louder than I thought it would, making me jump. I stared at it for a long time. I just had to light it on fire, or rip it apart, or something. I swallowed and marched over to it.

I grabbed a page. They were thick and textured. I began to tear. I fell to the floor, gasping as my sides felt like they were ripping apart. I breathed through it and grabbed the page to pull more, but had to stop again. I lifted up my shirt, panting. Three long, thin scratches traced their way across my ribs and down my side. They stung and seared with pain.

I shoved my shirt back down and went for the lighter. I held my breath, expecting to be scorched as I held the flickering flame to the book. Nothing happened. Neither that damned book nor myself were burned. Not one part of the cover blackened. Not a wisp of smoke. I opened the front cover to hold the flame closer to just one, single sheet. It cracked open to the page. That evil page that Donny had read and reread, had spoken and respoken. It laid there, tempting me to try, tempting me to reach out to Donny. I closed my eyes, not wanting my mind to process the words I saw. Behind closed lids, flashes of Donny's glistening teeth in his wide strangulation smile flooded. His teeth became slick with saliva and pointed. Fear propelled me out of the kitchen and into my bedroom.

I dug around and found a couple of black pens. I grabbed black sharpies and markers. I sprinted to the kitchen and ripped open the junk drawer and found more. With shaking hands, I snatched and almost dropped a large mixing bowl. I felt like I was being chased like I had to hurry before it knew what I was doing.

I unscrewed the end of the pens and pulled out the middles. I put the inner tube up to my mouth and sucked in, but it had been too hard. Ink splattered on my face and in my mouth. I spit it out in the bowl and added what was left from the tube. I did that with the next pen and the next pen. I grabbed the markers, held them over the bowl, leaned back with my eyes squeezed shut, and snapped them, mixing in their contents.

The apartment felt heavy, curious. I pressed through, even though my chest constricted. I staggered forward with the bowl of mixed inks in my hands and poured it across the opened book. Ink spread and consumed the words. I picked up the book by its nameless cover and allowed for the pages to hang down. A bubbly giggle rose out of me as I dipped it into the bowl of ink, its pages reluctantly soaked up the black. I jolted. There came a growl, deep and dying, from far away and yet right next to my ear. The weight on my chest subsided little by little. Whatever else was left in the book couldn't be read ever again. Not by me, not by Donny, not by another innocent person who was just trying to find some peace. I slumped to the floor as my giggles turned into sobs.

I sat there, tears and inky spit running down my face. My teeth were probably black and I looked at my stained hands. I was a mess, but I knew I was safe from the book and what was in it. Even if Gaspara was right, and there was nothing I could do for Donny, I could still prevent people from falling prey to whatever the fuck we had been exposed to.

"You were always so smart," Donny mumbles.

I was on my feet in an instant.

"You're smarter than anyone in our family," he said, with a sigh. "I never would have thought of that." He was crying in the living room.

I saw him, laying on the couch like how he always used to, in that depressed fetal position, unmoving.

"Wh-what are you do—"

"I never would have thought of that," he said again, this time in a whisper. "I'm so stupid."

"No," I say reaching out to him. "Donny, you're—"

And before I could touch his shoulder, his head snapped to me. Thick, black, ink tears oozed from his eyes as he looked to me. His eyebrows scrunched together, pained.

I screamed, and he vanished. Leaving me alone, once again.

I collapsed into sobs. Donny was out there floating or whatever ghosts do, waiting for his one last shot at redemption. He wasn't pleading for his afterlife, but I knew he deserved to have rest, and I was the only one that could help him.

"I'm doing it, Donny," I whispered. "I'm fucking doing it."

And it was that resolve that motivated me to forget my life, to drive his Jeep, to find that gate. It was knowing he deserved serenity that gave me purpose, gave me pull and helped guide me. It's how I am where I am. It's where I'm supposed to be. It's how I'll put him to rest.

I use Laken's steady pace and our rocking motion to lull me back to the present.

"We are going to a lake?" I ask to end the silence, to make me more mindful of my surroundings.

"Yes. Not just a lake, but *the* lake. It's the only one I know of in the woods. It's huge, and in the middle is The Mount. It's where that orange-red clay comes from for those visibility traps outside of camp and on our hides."

I nod and let myself sway in time with Laken's steps. I'm still not used to my short hair. I kept thinking bugs are on me as stray ends brush my shoulders.

"And that's where you found Laken?"

"More like Laken found me," Wyatt says leaning forward and patting Laken on her neck. She gives a little snort while she steadily moves onward. "Well, I was fishing, and I honestly thought she was a big fish. I tried to spear her."

I laugh. "I bet she loved that," I say, remembering how she destroyed the large, horned rabbit.

"You bet. Well, she pinned me all the way at the bottom of the lake. I thought I'd disappear for sure."

"How in the world did you get out of that?"

"I got lucky. I smashed a bunch of mud in her nose. She got off me just a little and then I tried to ride her. You know how I told you I grew up on a farm? Well, we had a couple horses and one had an attitude just like Laken here. So I got lucky again and stayed on."

"So we are going back to the place where Laken tried to kill you? Great plan," I say, smiling.

"You'll love it, but before we get there, I wanted to show you something else."

I fight the butterflies in my stomach as we get closer to a grove of tall pines. Their branches are so heavy with needles that they almost weep. They have something else on their limbs, weighing them down. A thick dusting of white coats each elongated branch. It's still and hopeful.

"Is that snow?" I ask.

"I thought so too, at first. They're actually what I wanted to show you."

We get closer and one of the branch's 'snow' is moving. Little white puffs bob around and cuddle next to each other. They're tiny birds, pruning and fluffing in clusters.

"They're birds?"

"Yep. Aren't they cute?"

"They look like little happy cotton balls." A giggle escapes my lips.

When we walk past a branch, they flutter away. They look like large, white bumble bees, fat with fuzz and stumpy wings. They can't fly very far and they have to flap their wings really hard.

"Yeah, they're a bunch of marshmallows and they love these big pine trees."

We ride further, and as the branches drift past, I try to look at each little bird, so content with its family. Near the end of the grove, there are fewer trees that give way to an expanse of meadow. There's a cloudy sky and bright sunlight. Even though it's overcast, it's almost blinding to be out under the sky without the thick arms of trees to shield us.

The meadow is teeming with wildflowers and butterflies. Some have long, curling antennae, while others are the size of my face and seem to flap in slow motion. They search for nectar and ignore us completely as we follow a narrow path that leads through the middle.

"I know it's a bit of a detour, but it's so beautiful and I want you to see that Hollow Forest isn't all bad," he says.

I reach out a hand and a shimmering green and purple one almost lands on me as we bob and sway. A few orange and white ones flutter close to my head. They remind me of butterfly kisses my mom used to give me when I was little. Laken snorts at a couple, and they flit away.

"Thank you," I say, and take in the purples, blues, and reds of endless wildflowers.

"Hang on." He leans over and snatches up a handful of flowers. "Here you go, m'lady," he says in a false British accent.

They're gorgeous snapdragons, windflowers, daisies, and grasses.

"Thanks," I say, not taking them. "You're so weird." I love them, roots, dirt clumps, and all. "I need to try that. I'm not good at the reaching thing yet."

I left him holding onto the bouquet of flowers. I lean over, keep a tight grip on Laken's mane, and grab at a few tall stems. I snap off some of the blooms and accidentally crumple them in my fist when I'm about to fall. I jolt upright and awkwardly strain to turn my body and face Wyatt. Laken sneezes in protest.

"Here you go. Do you love them?" I ask.

We laugh at the rumpled petals and yellow pollen smashed into my palm.

"Yes, absolutely," he says, and we both chuck the flowers back into the meadow, disturbing a cloud of butterflies.

It isn't long until we climb over the next rolling hill in the meadow that I gasp.

There it is. The Mount.

My heart wants to plunge from my chest and sore to the mountain. My legs demand to sprint in its direction. My arms spasm and jerk. My eyes flick and twitch. I finally have the pull. The Mount is where I have to go.

# CHAPTER TWENTY-THREE

THE MEADOW GIVES way to soft soil and rocks at the edge of the pristine lake. The water is a solid sheet of dark green, stained glass. I've missed the ocean. The lake doesn't have crashing waves, but it's a silent sea.

The water glistens and reflects The Mount at its center. It looms mysteriously, the lone monolith at the lake's heart. The rusty orange and rich red clay summit looks kaleidoscopic and twice the size it actually is. Its low ascent leads to a sheer face and flat top. It's relatively small, but it feels like it has eyes that watch us from far away.

Skeletor screeches and keeps his flight at a steady pace over the water and toward The Mount while Laken trots with excited steps.

"Is that bad? You said he would screech if things were bad."

"No. He's excited. He wants to have a dust bath in the clay. He does it to make himself feel vicious or something. He's actually white."

"No way! Skeletor puts on makeup?" I say, remembering the first time I saw Donny in guyliner. His makeup made him look and feel fierce. Skeletor deserved the same treatment, I supposed.

"Yes, exactly. It makes him feel good, I guess. And I admit, he does look pretty badass as an orange bird. It helps me see him better, too."

I smell the wet, overturned mud at the lake's edge when we get closer. Laken walks right into the water.

"Oh, we have to get off now," Wyatt says and quickly dismounts.

"What, why?" I scramble to get off as her front legs fold under her.

Laken lies right down in the water and flops on her side. Her gills appear and open. She sucks in water through her nose and it pours from her neck. She closes her eyes in pleasure. Her skin almost glows in the water. Wyatt bends down and pats her on the neck.

"Are you going to swim, girl? You can. Go get yourself some fish," he says.

She gets up slowly and wades into the water until she's completely submerged. The water closes over her head and sends ripples that grow wider and wider and extend into the far distance.

"I need to be there," I say.

"I wouldn't go swimming in there. It looks real nice, but there are lake monsters, eels, and all kinds of nasty things."

"No, not there." My eyes flick to see if there are any Fiends. Long, slithering shadows snake their way in and out of view. I shudder.

"Where?"

"The Mount. I have the pull again." I can't help but smile. I turn and look at Wyatt, who isn't smiling back. "You don't understand. It's been gone. I didn't have the pull at all after you disappeared, and I felt so lost."

"No, I know exactly what you mean. Remember? I told you that I usually don't have it until someone needs help. Like what I felt for you," he says.

"No. I know you said that, but this is different."

"Look, I'm not trying to tell you not to be excited, I just don't think it's a good idea. You need to learn a few more things first, and then maybe we can start planning on how to get there. But we need to wait until you're more ready," he says. He pulls a spear off his back and forces it into my hands.

"But, you said that if I don't listen to the pull, the Canid Carey can kill me. Then what?"

"No. What I was saying was that if your doubt and fear keep you from continuing, then you'll be hunted and consumed."

"Isn't that what you're telling me to do?"

"No, no it's not that. It's just that I don't think it would be a good idea to jump to The Mount right this second. I think that maybe it would be better if you would focus on honing your skills and we can do it together. You know? Like, so you aren't going in there blind."

He walks away from me, barefoot with the water already up to his knees. Although I appreciate his wisdom, I don't like how he's turning his back to me.

"Hey. I have a reason for this. I'm on a time limit. I get it. You want me to be more prepared or whatever. One thing I've learned here, though, is that I'm never going to be prepared. We could have the easiest plan in the world, like yesterday when we went to get water. And it could all get fucked. We honestly need to just go for it. Get supplies, sure, but get skills? What does that even mean?"

"Skill! Like, throwing a knife or knowing how to tie knots. You don't know how to do those things, and they could help you."

"I'm already cutting it close to my deadline," I say, thinking of my traumaversary. If time is even the same here, I have about three days to take his ashes to the top of that mountain. That's where my brother and I need to be.

"Deadline to what? Deadline to carrying a heavy-ass urn through the water and to a mountain where the Canid literally lives and can see you clearly? Or deadline to when you want to kill yourself?" His words shoot out at me and cut deeply.

"Whoa."

"I'm not saying this to scare you. I'm trying to be realistic. Take it from someone who has died trying – multiple times, mind you – to get to The Mount. And no offense, but I've been here a while, and if I can't do it yet. Well."

"How did you know?" I say.

"Know that the Canid lives there? Because you can see it stalking around. It's that clay stuff, like what I was telling you—"

"No. How did you know I have an urn I need to take with me?"

He stops roaming the water and looks at me.

"Wyatt." I spit out his name.

"I didn't want you to think I was going through your stuff."

"But you did?"

"But I did," he says, his voice quiet.

We both just look at each other. My voice quivers when I finally speak. "I know, in my heart, that I need to take my brother and scatter his essence at the top of that Godforsaken mountain, or I'll die trying. I came here knowing that I would probably never return. You dance around it all the time, but I'll probably become a Stain at some point."

"Don't say that," he says. His shoulders slump.

"Why? You said you wanted to be realistic, so let's be realistic.

155

I came here after my brother wanted to stop living because he got possessed or something. He was always chasing stuff. Heroin. His dead boyfriend. My parents' love. And it fucking killed him. He's dead, and I was kind of thinking he'd be at peace. But no – his chasing got him damned, and now it's my job to set him free. I was told I needed to take his essence to where my intuition took me. It's his last chance to rest in fucking peace, and it's up to me."

"No, it isn't."

"What? Are you going to lecture me on how it's his choices, or my parents' fault, or that he's just a lousy addict? He made his bed, so lie in it, right?"

"No, that's not what I'm—"

"No? Then what are you saying? Tell me. Whatever do you mean?"

"I'm just saying that you've made it here. You've thrived here, even. If we're being honest, no one usually lasts more than a week, two if they're lucky. Yet somehow, you've made it longer. And every single one of those lost people felt the need to go to this mountain. I thought that maybe, because you had lost your pull, like me, that the reason you made it was because you weren't drawn to that awful mountain. It's a death trap. It's like everyone in here is a moth and that's the flame. You'll just blindly follow. Did you ever stop to think that it's all a trick?"

Donny was so sure he spoke with Zach. How he swore by it, to the point he had let something evil take him over. I shake my head, trying to get the thoughts out.

"Don't shake your head. Think about it. I've lasted here, and I was never attracted to that awful mountain. That's what the Canid does. It helps you embrace it so it can terrorize you."

"I know, Wyatt. I know that. In case you forgot, I have been living with a demon vulture, a crazy skin horse, and waiting for a cloud man in a fucking skirt to come back. I've had my run-ins with the unexpected, and I know what the luring feels like. It's not the same. It feels completely different. What? Why are you smiling?"

"A cloud man in a skirt?" he snickers.

My lips turn up in a smile. "Stop! I'm just trying to—"

"First off, there's nothing wrong with skirts. They're roomy. Second of all, I fold it all up like a warrior princess and it works for me. Third of all, I know it's gross, but the Hollow turns you into a scavenger at some time or another. It's how you survive. But, I ran out of corpses to rob of clothing. The material just wasn't durable. So I made my own."

I look at my own clothes, torn, dirtied, and in ruins. The only things that remain put together are my hiking boots and the Owletta hide he made.

"You're right. That *is* gross," I laugh. "But a warrior princess has gotta do what a warrior princess has gotta do."

He splashes me. The cold water hits me in the face with a sharp slap.

"It's about time you get in this lake and stop yelling at me. Do you want to learn to fish or what? It's some good stuff. And with some reeds here, we can pretend we're eating sushi at a fancy restaurant."

I want to laugh. I want to run into the water, arms wide, and just hold him. I want something solid, tangible, sustainable. But it isn't him. It's myself and what I know to be true.

"I like that idea," I say, sitting down on the rocks and mud to take off my boots. "But, I'm going to that mountain."

"I know." He doesn't look at me.

"Like, I know that I need to go, and soon."

He's preoccupied with something apparently more important

in the water. I take off my boots and admire my calloused feet. They look so different than when I first found myself inside Hollow Forest. I walk into the water. The mud slips between my toes as I wade deeper. I jump when Laken appears out of nowhere and snorts water on us like a dolphin.

"Get out of here. Go catch some fish," Wyatt says, shaking one of the spears I made at her.

She soundlessly dips below the water again, disappearing in seconds.

"I think she already did."

"Nah. She's just showing off." He hands me another spear from his back. "The trick is to stand still and have some leverage. Like, bring it straight down. Laken helps because she has an attractant oil on her skin."

"Ew."

"It's not 'ew' if it's going to help us eat." He stabs the spear straight down on a fish that swims close to his ankles.

He draws it from the water and shows off his catch with a proud smile. The fish writhes and I have to look away. "What? It was a good kill."

"Yeah. I just kind of miss when I didn't know what my food looked like alive. I want to think of fish as actual sushi rolls, not one that's dying in front of me."

"It took me a while, too. But we've gotta eat," he says, already hunting for another.

# CHAPTER TWENTY-FOUR

WE FISH UNTIL the sun slowly descends. I've caught one compared to Wyatt's five. I'm proud of my puny fish with gray scales, though. I made its death swift and I keep whispering that I'm thankful for its sacrifice. I don't want to be a thoughtless Fiend, driven by my hunger. Wyatt strings up the six fish on my rope and splashes the water three quick times. I guess it's a signal to Laken so she'll come back to shore. She doesn't at first, and Wyatt gets agitated and looks at the sun setting behind the small, flat-topped mountain.

"Laken needs to get back here. We need to get home before it's too dark."

I fight the familiar terror rising in my chest. "Why?"

He ignores me and slaps the water three more times. She emerges slowly, taking her grand old time, plodding steadily from the water. The sun glistens off her skin and shines through the droplets streaming from her body. She shakes and whips her coarse mane and tail. We trudge out of the water and my hands are clumsy as I put my boots, hide, and mask back on. Wyatt does the same and transforms in front of my eyes from friend to Ruminant creature laden with the hide, fish, and spears.

He climbs on Laken and reaches a hand down for me. The setting sun fills me with dread. I don't want to leave the pull, and yet I need my brother before I go there. And there's no way I can navigate my way there at night.

"Wyatt?"

"Yes? Get on. Come on." He looks around, the reaching antlers of his mask swinging. Laken paws the earth.

"You said the split-faced kids were smart? But they didn't know that I was human," I say, one hand clutching Laken's mane and one hand in his. His palms and fingers are still wet and wrinkled from fishing.

"What I've found is that Fiends don't really see like you and I do," he says as I get comfortable and steal the reins from him. "They see fear and doubt. When we wear the hides and skulls, I think it either masks what we're feeling, or we are more confident wearing it. Can we pick up the pace?"

"Yeah. Geez. I don't feel confident with you flipping out."

"I'm not flipping out. I just don't want you to see—"

And that's when two people burst through the meadow, screaming for help and checking behind them. Laken keeps pace without acknowledging them. Wyatt slumps behind me. They are two guys bolting through the woods. One keeps looking over his shoulder and falls. His face bounces off the ground. His friend passes him and dives right into the water, never looking back. The guy who fell flops strangely. An echo of a Fiend pounces him. His back cracks and his eyes bug as his limbs go limp. His head rolls to the side and flops as he's dragged by his leg into the forest. Wyatt sniffs. It's the kind of sniff you make when you're trying to hide your tears. That's when I know that he's reliving the loss of someone he loves. That's when I know that Stain is Tyler.

The guy who swims looks like he's good at it. He takes the

appropriate breaths, moves his arms and legs in synchronization. He makes it a decent distance out into the water before yelling that something touched his leg. He's pulled under and becomes no more than a ripple and crimson water.

We go through the rolling meadow and ride back into the forest, as if we hadn't just seen people's most terrifying moments on repeat. As if we hadn't just witnessed actual deaths. Was it old? Was it recent? Did it matter?

As we plod through the forest, screams and splashes echo. Hordes of Stains run into the wildflower meadow. They try to swim to The Mount. They force themselves to follow the pull, despite their fears, and they fail. Every single one of them fails, and are condemned to Hollow Forest forever. And I'm about to do the same fucking thing.

# CHAPTER TWENTY-FIVE

OUR DINNER PREP is filled with silence. Wyatt is tense and filets the fish with jerking movements and slices off the scales a bit too roughly. He curses about missing Charm and having to use City, even though they're practically the same knife. We wrap our raw fish in seaweed and I chew slowly, trying to focus on the delicious fish in my mouth instead of my fear about tomorrow. My throat is tight and I have to chew the meat into tiny bites so that I can actually swallow. Wyatt barely eats at all.

Laken's already asleep standing up and Skeletor is out on a nightly hunt. Wyatt looks like he's about to say something, but doesn't. I try to lighten the tension by talking about something, anything.

"So, you said that you have some acidic stuff? I think I saw you use it for Laken or something?"

"Yeah. It's a root. It helps me clean her wounds and helps her heal faster if she has a cut. I tried it on my own cuts to help, but it just hurts like hell and I still mist anyway."

I nod. "Have you ever tried to eat it? Like, could you eat it?"

"I guess. It should be okay," he says. "I mean, it works on cuts so it goes in the bloodstream and I've used it on ulcers in my mouth before. I've swallowed little bits of it by accident. It doesn't taste really good, though. Did you want to drink it or something? You're welcome to use it to swish out your mouth, but I suggest not drinking it."

"Actually, I was going to try something on my little fish I caught."

"Um, sure."

When he comes back from the branch dome, he has a smaller bladder that holds the red liquid in it. When he sits next to me and opens it up, it looks like tomato juice. Wyatt shows me how to skin my tiny fish and then I plop it into the acid.

"That's starting to look like some bad soup," he says.

"No, I'm not going to drink it, but I want to cook it."

"Yeah. I get tired of raw stuff, too. But fires don't start here."

I roll my eyes. "Well, I know that. I'm trying to see if this makes ceviche."

"Sev what?"

"Seh-veech-ay," I say. "It's a Peruvian thing. You use the acidity from lemons to cook raw fish."

"Oh, fancy." Wyatt finally smiles for the first time tonight. "You visit Peru or something?"

"Yeah. I have a couple times."

"Oh-ho, fancy-pants world traveler over here."

"Well, I like traveling, but my mom's family lives there. I don't know why I didn't think of this before."

"Tell me about it."

"About what?"

"About Peru. Your family. The world the last time you left it."

"Oh. I didn't think you liked hearing about that stuff."

"Well, I don't usually. It just makes me homesick for a place I can't get back to. This is my home now, and I've grown to love it." He has a sad smile on his face. "But I want to know more about you," he says.

I want to ask why, when I would leave tomorrow. I don't want to leave him with empty shadows of what the outside world is. I don't want him to get to know me. I don't want him to miss me. But against my better judgment, I tell him about Peru, and its breathtaking mountains, and Machu Picchu. I tell him about living near the ocean and how much I miss it. I tell him about my distant parents and how my brother's the only family I've ever felt unconditional love for and from. How Donny was tricked by that evil book, and why I'm fighting against time. Wyatt tears up when I bring up my family and a part of me wants to ask him more. But a larger part of me doesn't want to know about him. I don't want yet another reason to stay. I'm tempted enough as it is.

"I can tell you love your brother a lot," he says.

"Yes, and I miss him like crazy." My voice catches. "And all the awful stuff he's done because of his addiction really wasn't him, you know? Not the Donny I knew. And even in the middle of his disease and suffering, he still loved me and cared about me as much as he could. So you understand why I need to do this. You get how it's his last hope."

"Yes. I do understand."

"How did you get here, anyway?" I ask.

"I honestly don't know," Wyatt says and takes a peek at the little fish. "I remember going for a drive. I was going to meet my friends at this campsite, and then I was here."

It was just like how I got here. A car ride through the woods. But why couldn't Wyatt remember the gate?

"It should be done by now," I say. "It takes about thirty minutes to fully 'cook' in the acidity."

I tear off a piece and take a bite. My nose scrunches when

the sourness hits me, but it's really good. I hand him the rest of the fish to eat.

"That didn't look like it tasted very good," he says. Weirdly, he's hesitant.

"Just try it," I say.

He takes a bite. His face scrunches like mine, but as he chews he seems pleased.

"Not bad," he says, still thoughtfully chewing.

"It's better than that!"

"I've missed cooked food so much," he says and closes his eyes. "I had no idea you could do this."

I can't help but be proud. This way, if I become a Stain tomorrow, then I'd at least be able to give back to a guy who has been so generous to allow me to live here. He's offered his home, resources, and a way to survive, and I'm leaving him with nothing. Nothing but another Stain reminder on repeat.

"Yeah. Pretty cool how it works, right?"

"Yeah."

We both looked at each other for a long time, smiling our sad smiles and full from our catches of the day. After we wrap up the fish in salt and seaweed, we bed down. I lay down first and Wyatt puts a fur hide on me. I nestle myself in while he ties his dreads with a leather strip. He gets a fur to lay outside next to Laken.

"Where are you going?" I ask, propping myself up on my arm.

"Out by Laken so you can get your rest."

"I thought you'd stay here." My face grows hot and I'm thankful for the darkness.

"You don't mind?"

"Of course not. I liked it better when you stayed here last night."

"Yeah?"

"Yeah. I know if a Fiend breaks in here, they'll eat you first."

He laughs. "Oh, I see how it is."

Wyatt lays down and drapes his hide over himself. We rest there in silence, listening to the evil things scratch, sniff, and crawl around the outside of camp, oblivious to us just inside the tree dome.

"Aren't you scared?" Wyatt asks. There's hesitance in his voice.

"Yeah, of course. I've been scared since I got here."

He sighs. It's a desperate kind of sigh, one that's forced so he doesn't hold his breath.

"But you know what?" I say.

"What?"

I feel his heat. He's so close to me. The smell of earth and grasses radiates from his skin. He still has the faint aroma of the flowers in the meadow and the water from the lake. The split-face kids are right. He's a wild man, in a way that belongs in Hollow Forest.

"I also never have felt more at home. I know we are surrounded by things I don't totally understand, but having you has helped me so much. I know I wouldn't be alive without you." I scoot closer to him and reach out. I hug him, and he hugs me back. His heart beats against my chest. It's fast.

"I felt the pull for the first time in a long time with you. I think you're something spectacular," he whispers. His breath feels hot on my ear and his arms are warm around me.

I've never been called spectacular before. The little part of me that always bats away compliments, the one that's more comfortable with condemnation, actually believes that he's being genuine. It kind of makes me have faith that I can do something great tomorrow.

I lean back a little bit. I touch my nose to his. Our breaths are hot. I tilt my head and we kiss.

It's so easy, so smooth to slip into kissing him. He's soft, gentle, and it's like I've known him before. It's natural to kiss him.

His hands travel lower on my back and I take off my shirt, wanting as much of my skin to touch him. One of his hands caresses my face. It electrifies my cheek. I lean in closer, pressing my hips against his, not close enough.

"Wait," he says, a little breathless. "I don't, I mean I want to make sure everything is okay. What are, are you, are you alright? Is this okay?"

I always feared this moment. Am I doing this for control? To have a way to handle my own destiny when I know I may have less than a day to live? Is it because he's convenient? Would he drift into thinking of Chelsea, or Tyler, when he's with me?

And would I know what to do? Would Jacob take over my thoughts and not only destroy my very first romantic relationship but all the relationships after him? Would it hurt? Would I be scared?

And I do feel scared. I'm petrified.

But I don't hesitate. I want Wyatt. He is what's right, and decent, and unconditionally caring. He's my hope, and I want all of him.

"Yes," I say, shifting on top, kissing each cheek, kissing his neck, kissing his collar bone.

He moans and in seconds we are both naked and pressed against each other. He brushes back my short hair that keeps getting in the way. I snake my fingers through his dreads. We kiss and I feel his tongue in my mouth, his lips soft, his breaths even and reassuring. His kisses evolve further as we feel each other. The earthy moss and leaves crunch under us as we join together, our bodies in rhythm. I feel powerful with my hands on his chest and as my hips ride and plunge. He and I are partners, fully and truly. I trust him with my life, and he trusts me. When we each climax, pleasure cascades over me. We hold each other in bliss until I drift off, my heart content, my soul at peace.

# CHAPTER TWENTY-SIX

I wake up and my stomach flies to my throat as if I'm on a rollercoaster.

Wyatt is gone, and I'm alone and vulnerable in the moss bed.

I can't figure out what woke me until there's a steady sound of—what is that? Digging?

I shiver as I stand up. I scurry to cover my bare skin with clothes that were carelessly tossed aside. I run outside, bleary-eyed and sick. Laken is no longer snoozing. Her ears tilt and flick. Skeletor is perched high in the treetops, his head is cocked and his icy eyes focus on something on the far edge of camp, close to the tree with the large notch in it. I sneak closer and rage fills me. It's like a fire that licks my insides. I quake so deeply my bones are vibrating.

Wyatt's on his hands and knees. He uses Totto to hack and scrape at the ground and then he digs out the loose earth with his hands. He's making a hole. It's at least a foot deep, maybe even two. He's burying something. I crane my neck and a glint of silver catches my eye. Wyatt is putting my brother in the ground. The top of the urn is just barely visible.

"Hey. What the fuck are you doing?" I scream, running at him.

I want to shove him, kick him, bite him for trying to kidnap my brother. I want to make him bleed. And not his stupid mist, either, real blood with real consequences. I sprint at him, ready to pounce. His sable eyes grow wide when I run at him. He can't move quickly enough. Where just hours earlier I touched him so gently and eagerly, I now tackle him, screaming at the top of my lungs. He smacks down on his back in a flurry of limbs and groans.

"Angela, no. Stop." He's tired, deflated.

Skeletor lets out a long whistle.

"Stop? All you say is keep going, and now you're telling me to stop?"

I smash the palm of my hand into his nose, not realizing how strong I've become over the past few weeks. His nose cracks and he howls. Mist tumbles from his nostrils. His eyes water and there's a bit of guilt. An ache washes over me. I want to hit him again, but it's like I'm filled with lead.

I force myself to slide off him. I don't realize I'm crying until a sob wracks through me. I crawl over to my poor brother, already half-buried in the dirt. I pull him out. His urn's intricate silver markings are caked with soft soil that clings to the etchings. I hug him close to me, wishing he can say something stupid or just hug me back.

"Angela, I—"

"No." My voice is high and grates over my vocal cords. "Don't." I can't catch my breath.

My sobs echo into the slight dawn light while Wyatt's nostrils puff smoke. He tries to cover his nose, but the mist just seeps between his fingers and pools on the ground.

He walks on his knees over to me, reaching out a hand to my shoulder. I flinch and shrug him away.

"Angela, I couldn't let you do it."

"Let me?"

"No, I mean, you can't go. You've thrived here. You and I are a team. I didn't mean for you to see all those Stains yesterday by the lake, but now you know that—"

"Didn't you?"

"What?"

"You said you didn't mean for me to see the Stains by the lake, but now I think you did. You thought you could scare me out of it. But you can't stop me. I know what I need to do."

"And what is that? Get to the top of that fucking mountain? Do you know how many times I've heard excuses as to why they need to get to the mountain? To find the one true love. To find happiness. To change their luck. To cure their mom's cancer. To bring back their dead dog. To live forever."

"Excuses? This is my brother. He's—"

"Dead! Your brother is fucking dead."

"No."

"He is, Angela. He's nothing more than a pile of ash that you're going to lug to the top of a Stain-infested mountain where everyone else wanted to go."

"He's not dead."

"How can you say that when you are holding his literal ashes in your hands?"

"That's the problem. He's not dead. He's stuck in an in-between. Didn't you listen to anything I said? Or do you just assume you know everything all the time?"

"No, I'm hearing you, I just don't believe it. Have you heard from him since you got to Hollow Forest? How do you know those sight ladies or whatever didn't set you up?"

"They didn't."

"But how do you know? And the *really* ironic thing," he was shouting at me now, "is that if you decide to go on a suicide mission to the fucking Mount, then you'll be fucking stuck, too."

Skeletor screeches and hops on the branch, obviously upset.

I shake my head. "You just don't get it." My voice matches his level.

"Stop," he says.

"No, I won't. I haven't changed my mind. I'm going. And I can't believe I trusted you. I can't believe you got me to believe a fucking word you said."

"Stop talking." He raises a hand.

"I won't, Wyatt. You know all this shit about me and I don't even know your full na—"

"No. I mean it." His eyes dart. His body stiffens. "Quiet," he hisses.

I stop and my skin prickles. There's a light knocking on trees, a rustle of branches. Something is climbing in the trees to avoid being scorched on the ground by diamonds. There's shushing and slight giggles. It's an ambush.

We both stay crouched and creep our way back to the tree dome. The sound is coming from the entryway of the marked trees. I keep Donny clutched to my chest as Wyatt scurries ahead. He peeps around the dome.

"Shh, they are yelling. Follow me, Canid Carey. Don't touch the trees until I knock knock knock. Wild Man and Sad Lady are in here." There is a high, wheezing laugh.

"It's that last split-faced kid." Wyatt crouches back down and whispers to me. "The one with the long hair? You cut off its ear.

It's in the tree. It's not even trying to keep itself invisible. It must have been stalking us and found out how to lift the fog. They have us cornered."

Laken prances and snorts. Her ears turn and her milky eyes roll. There's sniffing and panting from the Canid. I imagine it salivating at the thought of consuming us. The wet fur smell is overpowering and I try not to gag. Wyatt probably can't smell it. There's still a puff or two of mist that occasionally swirls from his nostrils. I focus on my breathing and the weight of Donny's urn in my arms. I focus on the solidity of it and the pattern of hoof beats Laken makes.

Wyatt and I sneak into the tree dome, communicating through nods and eye movements. We grab a few spears, our knives, and Laken's bridle. I gently place Donny in my pack and cinch it securely to my back. I walk as low to the ground and as silently as possible, even though my heart thrums. The hissing giggles of the split-faced kid echo.

I slip the bridle on Laken. Her muscles are tense with adrenaline, ready for a swift getaway. I lead her back behind the dome, the only thing tall enough to block her. Skeletor flaps his wings and makes long whistles above us as we all cower. We don't dare get on her back. We don't want the Fiends to locate us.

Skeletor takes flight soundlessly and must be pecking at the split-faced kid because it says, "No birdie. Bad birdie."

The branches rustle more fervently.

They were so close now. How far along were they? Why hadn't Wyatt created a back door? We are just sitting ducks, waiting for them to get us.

"We can't just wait here to get killed," I say. There's an allure to run and greet the Canid Carey. To just get it over with. Wouldn't it be so relieving?

"It's already messing with me," I say, gagging on its putrid, rotting smell.

"There's only one way out," Wyatt says, trying to sneak a peek over the tree dome.

"Yeah, and they opened it wide for us. We just need to get out. On the count of three we are going to hop up on Laken and make a run for it," I say.

"Right to them? No. We need to wait until they come for us," he says.

"Okay, then that's what we'll do. One."

The branches sway.

"Two."

Skeletor cries and I imagine the release of running to the Canid Carey.

"Three."

I grab Laken's mane and swing up. I grip Wyatt's hand and we both mount. The Canid rushes at us, a silent and invisible brute force. I'm dizzy with visions of rotten flesh and sweet, thick blood. Of an eagerness to be wild and fling myself into its acrid disillusion. I still can't detect it. It keeps itself unseen as it catapults toward us. Laken's able to sense where it leaps and she sidesteps, jumping out of the way. Both of us almost slip off. The Canid crashes into the dome. Branches fly and snap on impact from its massive weight. It looks like an explosion. Moss, spears, splinters, and pelts shoot everywhere. Dirt kicks up in long scratches where the Canid Carey pivots to face us again. Laken screams and races to the opening.

We bolt toward the marked trees, Skeletor already pecking and flapping at the split-faced kid. Its jaw is unhinged and its rows of sharp teeth snap at Skeletor. There's something black and glistening in its hand. It's Charm, looking large in its tiny, emaciated fist. It curls back, ready to cut at Skeletor.

Wyatt whistles one long note that starts high and lowers. Skeletor flies lower with the sound. He forgets the split-faced kid and swoops to our level when we are at the edge of camp. We have to go under the branch the kid is sitting on. Wyatt tightens his legs, urging Laken to go faster. The kid is nearly on top of us.

"So sharp." It hisses and lets go of Charm as we run below. The blade bolts straight down, right at us.

"Charm, no," I rasp, causing Laken to kick up her heels even faster. The blade hovers in mid-air.

"Charm, reverse," Wyatt says.

The blade flips on end and shoots right back at the split-faced kid.

The knife thunks as it strikes the Fiend child and its little body thuds to the ground. Shivers run down my spine and I grit my teeth when the howl of the Canid starts at its shrillest and sinks into a deep bass. My eardrums buzz like they're about to pop. Its footfalls pound behind us.

Laken expertly zig-zags. I lean over, whack a tree trunk and Wyatt gets a slap in. It isn't the rule of three, but it has to do. The Canid is in for a rude awakening when it hits the partially closed Fiend screen. It could buy us some time, and that's all we need.

Just a little bit more time.

# CHAPTER TWENTY-SEVEN

I STEER LAKEN toward The Mount. Wyatt grips her mane with one hand and a spear with the other. He bumps against my pack, shoving Donny into my shoulder blades. My hands cramp as I grip the reins and lean forward. We are a team. Skeletor flaps low in front of us. We all know where we need to be. I can't help but smile when the yowl and whimpers of the Canid echo to us when it's caught in the Fiend screen.

"Ha. We got it, at least for a little bit," Wyatt says, his mouth next to my ear.

There are pants and heaves on both sides. I look, only to see a young boy, his Stain faded and worn, be swept off his feet and his neck snapped. On my left, a middle-aged man screams as his face is clawed open. Blood pours between his fingers as he tries to hold his lacerated flesh together.

I squeeze my legs tighter. Laken runs with bounding, thundering strides. I don't check behind me. Only forward.

We get to the meadow much faster this time without the detour. It's different at dawn. There are no butterflies and all of the flowers are still closed in the faint, pink light. We trample the stems and buds as we race to the water. Laken screams with joy when her hooves pound the rock and mud, kicking clumps behind her. When she makes her first splash into the water, she doesn't hesitate. But neither does the Canid Carey.

For the first time, I look behind us. Wyatt does, too. He jumps off Laken's back when the water gets up to her belly.

"What are you doing?"

"Go, go." He tosses the spear from one hand to another, steeling himself. "He can't get me and I can hold him off, for at least a little bit."

"With a tree branch?" I yank on the reins to hold Laken back.

The flowers get trampled from the invisible enemy. Huge patches are smashed as it leaps toward us. It's gaining, and fast.

"It's after you, not me. Go now. And let Laken do whatever she needs to. She knows how to survive." He smacks her hindquarters, sending her jolting forward.

I almost fall off of her again as we plunge into the lake. The water hits my shins and then up my thighs as she submerges. She moves differently in the water. Her body is slick and cutting. Her skin is slippery and slimy, like an eel's. As she moves deeper, I lift off her back. I kick my legs, splashing while Laken slithers.

I gasp when a Stain's arms splash and reach above the water, only to be towed under. I cling tighter as their last breaths bubble. What took them under? In the distance are more Stains swimming, all grasping, panting, kicking to just reach The Mount.

I catch a mouthful of green water when she ducks under. The lake's surface smacks my face. We go deep and then come back up. I cough and sputter out a mouthful of water. My neck strains to keep my head afloat. What the Hell was that about? Were those Stains dragged under by something I couldn't see? Or was it a kelpie, just like the one I'm putting my trust into now? Before I catch a breath, we dive under again, even deeper this time. She twists and I'm only clutching her mane with one hand. I kick to try and get back on, but she resurfaces faster than I swim. I grip her hair with my fist while her wild, sightless eyes roll. Water streams and spurts from gills in her neck. I cough more and suck in as much as I can. Is she trying to drown me like she did with Wyatt the first time he rode her?

We're halfway to The Mount. I look back at the shore. Wyatt circles the invisible monster. His spear keeps it at bay. He backs into the water and pokes at the air. Skeletor emits horrid screeches while he watches everything unfold from an aerial view. His cries are muted when we plunge underwater once more.

I'm ready for it this time. I clutch her mane with both hands and only let a little air escape my lips. Wyatt said to go with Laken and follow her lead. I open my eyes and there's a huge shadow. It looks like a sunken log until it twists to face us. It has a long snout, like a crocodile's, and many teeth. Its skin has thick, dark scales. It has six legs that work rhythmically to propel it. It swims a half-circle around us. Its long, spiked tail acts as a rudder to make it twist and turn. It lunges and a scream emerges from my lips as bubbles. My screech resonates through the water, making the monster's movements jolt and twist even faster, excited by its prey.

Laken darts out of the way. I have to kick with her to keep my grip. The monster snaps where we just were, its teeth vibrating. We swim higher before Laken drives down, her front hooves pointed at its head. It swims away with that same snaking motion. She slams her hooves into its back. It turns its ugly head, opening its mouth wide before going deeper into the murky, green waters. Laken lets out a high-pitched cry. She isn't letting it go.

My lungs are on fire as we plunge deeper. The water swirls in cold currents when we shoot into the depths. I focus my tight grip on her mane, the only thing keeping me alive. My ears pop with each charge. I get a glimpse of its massive silhouette again through the turbid water. We surge. This time, Laken hits her mark, screeching the entire time.

Her hooves strike at the base of its neck at an impossible speed. It cracks and the impact vibrates through my body. It's killed instantly. She turns in a flurry of bubbles and races for air. I don't have much time.

Water streaks past my face. My grip loosens with hands that are numb from the cold. When we break the surface, I gasp. I can't get enough air into my lungs. My vision is speckled with black splotches and my hands clumsily hold on while Laken swims directly for The Mount. My arms ache from clutching and my legs are like rubber. I have to keep kicking so that Laken's current won't separate me from her.

When Laken's hooves hit the rocks on the shore, warm tears streak my face. She trots out of the water and I'm paralyzed by the sudden weight of gravity. I lay across her back, my arms outstretched and hands cramped. My legs dangle over her haunches. She shakes the water off her body and I slip right off her slimy back and crash onto the rocks. Totto bruises my hip where it's sheathed and the urn clangs against the pebbled ground.

My elbow throbs as I rip open my backpack. The smelly lake water streams down my arms. I inspect my brother's urn. The duct tape has somehow held, though it's bubbled and warped. I tug at the lid and it's stuck tight. It will have to do.

I clamber with the backpack and my brother secured on wobbly, tired legs. I turn to look at the shore. It appears deceptively closer than it actually is. Wyatt's in the lake up to his knees. The beast splashes, encircling him. It's a smart move. He found a way to detect where the Canid Carey actually is, but his movements are delayed by the water. He whistles and whistles. Skeletor screeches overhead and zooms down at him, only to return overhead and circle.

Finally, one of the whistles sounds again and Skeletor dives. His talons grip Wyatt's arms. I'm in awe as Skeletor flaps hard, slowly ascending while clutching Wyatt. I wince as the splashes reveal the Canid's movements. Water sprays onto Skeletor. He flaps and tries to gain altitude.

Wyatt throws the spear at the Canid.

It makes Skeletor lurch, but it strikes its mark. The beast howls that ear-splitting cry. The attack gives Wyatt just a few seconds to get out of range.

I hug myself as they soar to us. Wyatt yells something, but I can't tell what he's saying. A cloud of billowing, smoky mist trails after his body. His back is in tatters. "Go," Wyatt screams.

Laken dances on the rocks and whinnies a response to his cries. Her excitement increases as they get closer and closer.

"It's coming. Run," he yells.

There's movement in the lake. Splashes and ripples show the invisible creature still charging our way. It swims with broad strokes. Laken still prances and neighs. Skeletor works hard to travel with Wyatt, but his talons tear at Wyatt's shoulders and he can't fly any higher.

"Laken, come on." I grip her mane and reins again. My elbow is sore and when I try to jump on her back, my legs are useless. I can barely leap and she sidesteps me, trying to call to her master.

"Laken," I say. My voice comes out hoarse and the salt from my streaming tears slide into my mouth.

I catapult myself with what energy I have left. My brother slaps against my back when I finally climb on. Laken doesn't want to go. I squeeze my legs and she just backs up, edging into the water.

"Go," Wyatt screams again. He's practically on top of us.

The Canid is close now, three-quarters of the way to shore, and Laken doesn't care. She just wants Wyatt.

I click my tongue, dig my heels into her side, and lean far forward. It propels her to walk, then trot, then lope up the side of the steep mountain where a thin trail leads the way. Laken kicks up the red soil and scant, dry grass as we follow the path. It eases its way up the mountain, trying to make the ascent more manageable. Laken slips and I bump forward, expecting to fall at any second. She catches herself, though. Skeletor drops a limping Wyatt onto the rocky shore behind us.

I stop Laken to let her take a breath. She's heaving hard. All that work to get up the mountain and we're only about a quarter of the way there. Wyatt rests his hands on his knees as mist pours from his back. He'll probably start disappearing soon. He's giving off so much smoke. He won't be able to last. His cloud hovers close to the ground, creating a fog around his ankles. It travels out to the lake and rolls among the giant ripples and splashes that are much too close. Water and foam spray on shore.

And that's when I finally see it. The Canid Carey.

# CHAPTER TWENTY-EIGHT

ITS MASSIVE CLAWS, long and sharp, appear as it reaches the red and rocky shore. They connect to thin, spindly fingers. Its humanoid arms are matted with sparse rusty brown fur. It emerges from the water, snarling. Its eyes are empty, black sockets. They swirl like dying stars. The Canid Carey has a long, thin muzzle that foams like a rabid dog's. Its lips curl back, revealing yellowed teeth. It's emaciated and disproportionate. Its arms and shoulders sit much higher than its short, powerful haunches, its oily smell detectable from where we stand. Each spinal bone protrudes their way down its back to its long, bristled tail that hangs low, unusually bent. Its ribs heave, threatening to pierce through the skin. Laken breathes heavily, not needing to see the Fiend to be terrified.

It towers over Wyatt, who can only stare. Smoke flows from his back and makes his shoulders fade away. The Canid licks its lips and howls. It rings so loudly my ears might explode. It echoes over the lake, past the rolling wildflower meadow, and into the forest. It rattles through me, making me purposeless. Why am I even here? For Wyatt to have a horrible death again? To take some ashes to the top of a mountain?

Water streams from the Canid as it lurks over to Wyatt. It's toying with its prey. It laps at the smoke, tasting him, feeding off him. I take in a sharp breath and panicked thoughts stab at me. What if the Canid kills Wyatt and it's his real death? What if he ceases to exist if he's devoured? What would happen if the beast consumes his mist? It's so hungry for him.

Wyatt's on his side in the rocks with the Canid lapping at his smoke, hunched over him, its lips curled back into a sinister smile. The Canid's head is bent low, making its shoulders protrude even more like a hyena. Wyatt struggles to move. He must be overcome with thoughts to join the dead because one second he reaches a hand up as if to lovingly stroke its sneering, putrid muzzle, and the next he hurriedly scoots away.

Wyatt's doing this so I can get to the top. I don't want his death to be in vain, but I don't want to leave him. I can't shake the nagging sense of dread. What would happen if Wyatt welcomes his own death to such an ancient, hungry creature?

The Canid still gets close, even when I'm calm. When it howls, I'm saved by Wyatt every time. That beast randomly and obsessively comes after me. But no. It isn't after me. The Canid is after Wyatt. It's *always* been Wyatt.

A horde of Stains, some fresh and vibrant, others aged and translucent, scream and scurry to climb The Mount. Some are slaughtered before my eyes, while others rush past me. But I know how they end. I won't watch their deaths.

I turn Laken, knowing that I need to act fast. I can't leave him to fight this alone. He can't die. As if reading my mind, Laken descends The Mount in sprints, pummeling through the onslaught of panicked Stains. The thought of making it to the flat top of the mountain is whisked away as the wind whips my hair.

The dark eye sockets, as vacant as nothing, glare at me. There's an emptiness at what existence would be if it just ended. It's not an easy, peaceful death luring me back anymore. It's fear, coldness, and isolation that will last a thousand years. A void of nothing at all. It tells of nothing before and nothing to come. Of no life lived, and of no remembrance hereafter.

I focus on Laken's solid steps, on the rocks that crack and fly from under her hooves. We cut through the cool winds. I raise Totto above my head, and I scream as loudly as I can.

Its lips peel back further. Horrid breaths huff through rotting, sharp teeth. It howls again, making my ears ring. Its greasy fur shines slick and clumped. It squares up with me and Laken, ready.

Laken has just one misstep. She hesitates for a second, and the Canid attacks. It swipes at her with its claws. She sidesteps the attack, her keen senses allowing her to keep us safe. I move with her and never lose my balance. I slice at its outstretched arm, hacking a clump of fur and flesh away. I gag as its brown, sludgy fluids bleed from it. It smells of rotten meat.

The Canid Carey lets out a moan that rattles my chest. Despite Wyatt's feeble cries to go on without him, I turn Laken and she paws the ground. We charge forward and the Canid swipes, this time making contact with Laken, sending us gasping and reeling to the ground. I fall on my side, sending shockwaves up my elbow and hip. I wheeze as I struggle to get my legs under me. The urn clangs against my back.

Laken was thrown into the water. Three long gashes rip across her side. Her blood pools, turning the water around her dark red. Ripples form in the middle of the lake when scaly tails and long, ridged backs rise out of the water in arcs before disappearing. There are more of those monsters, and they're stirring now that they have a taste of her blood. Laken sloshes in the water, trying to get away. She's too badly scratched. She hides her face under the murky water, breathing it in and listening for her predators' arrival.

I struggle to my feet, my knees and back buckling in protest. My wrist throbs where I was holding Totto. I grip my machete again and stagger toward the Canid Carey's back. It's facing away from me, the allure of Wyatt's white smoke too much. He's mostly dissipated except for an arm and the bottom half of his face.

I scramble over the rocks, covering ground faster than I thought I could, gritting my teeth against the ache in my bones. All I see is red. Red blood. Red anger. Red mountain. I plunge Totto into the Canid Carey's back, so far that it sticks in its rib cage. I cling to Totto, trying to yank it out. It's stuck, held fast, and so am I. My whole body whips as the Canid Carey tries to shake me off its back. It splashes in the lake water, the putrid wet dog smell washing over me. It arches and I leap out of the way when it falls on its back to crush me. Instead, it only succeeds in driving Totto in further.

The monster howls again as the inky, textured ooze pours out around the blade, reeking of rotting death. He bleeds into the lake. The slithering, ridged backs of the lake monsters refocus their attention. There are so many of them. Some peek slitted eyes above the water at a potential dinner.

I run to Laken, trying to drag her to her feet.

She snaps at me and pants heavily as she tries to stand. Her eyes are half-closed and she huffs, trying to get to her feet. She stumbles and falls into the water with a grunt. She kicks at a monster that's much smaller than the others, but with just as many rows of teeth. It backs away from her hind legs. It hisses, its mouth agape. She flops around like a fish and disappears beneath the surface of the lake. I'm left with only her blood-ied water.

One of the lake monsters, with dull scales, glaring eyes, and open jaws, crawls its way on the shore and snaps its pointed teeth. The Canid Carey hunches on all fours. Its head is low as it snarls at the reptile. More monsters swarm the Canid. It yelps when one lunges. The Canid's splashing frenzy only excites them.

While the Canid's preoccupied, I run to Wyatt. He's only a shoulder and lower face. I fight my urge to run away from his dismembered body. I kneel down in his cloud next to him, my hands shaking as I touch his cheeks. They turn to mist. I inadvertently speed up the dissolving process.

"Go," he mouths. "Go now."

With tears in my eyes, I run with everything I have. I follow the little trail and have to crawl on all fours at some points up The Mount's steep slope. Its red clay smears up my arms and under my fingernails. I can't grip anything correctly. I stumble up. The splashing and growling behind me gets louder. When I can't run or climb any more, I rest my hands on my knees, doubled over and panting. I'm much higher than before. Wyatt's nowhere in sight. He's completely mist by now, in whatever cold, white world he goes to. But at least he's safe.

The Canid still has Totto lodged in its back but ignores it. He swipes at the monsters and sends one spiraling through the air. With a splash, it lands in the lake. The Canid lunges at another, lips curled, its sinewy muscles taut. In a swift movement, it bites the largest of the monsters by its stout neck and shakes. It's limp, dead weight in its jaws. The lake monsters scuttle away. They fade into the depths, fearful of the Canid's power.

It drops the monster on the rocks, belly up, and tears at its throat. It isn't satisfied until the jugular is severed. The monster's heart still beats and bathes the Canid Carey's muzzle in blood. The red is bright and vibrant against its ruddy, dark brown fur. Slowly, slowly, its sockets raise and target me. I can't keep myself from staring into them. Even that far away, the void reaches out and sends ice down my spine. The beast throws back its head and howls, victorious and on the hunt once more. I sprint.

My lungs are on fire. The heavy footfalls thud and rocks spray and clatter behind it. I tell myself to focus on the flat top, my goal. The thin trail becomes non-distinct and I finally run up to the face of the plateau. It looms straight above me. I won't have to climb for long, but I can't lose my grip.

Two Stains, a man and a woman with toned arms and gritted teeth, are clinging to the ledge of The Mount's abrupt drop. They must have followed a different path, because they climb and sway over the cliff side of the red mountain. The man yelps and I think he'll hang on, but he inevitably drops silently onto the rocky shore below. I don't know what's worse – his silent death, or the horrible sound that screeches from his partner's mouth as she watches him die right before she too slips and succumbs to the same fate.

I grab onto a ledge above my head. I can't think about what I saw. My fingers barely hold it. I have to stand on the tips of my toes when I put each foot shakily on a thin ledge. My hand slips and I fall to the ground. I land on my feet. I wipe my palms on my filthy shirt, an attempt to dry the sweat. The strike of the Canid Carey's claws is enough motivation for me to try again.

I gulp and steady my breathing, and I grip the ledges once more. Instead of climbing straight up, I scoot to the side. It crumbles under my feet, forcing me to continue. Where once the climb was gradual, it's now a sheer face. I edge around the circumference and hang over the cliff. I glance down for a second and my world spins. The lake is further below me than I thought. I try to climb upward. There's a better place to grab and pull myself higher. The Canid howls again, making my ears vibrate. It's so close, sniffing where I was standing moments ago. I won't look down. Only the flat top holds my attention.

I climb, ignoring the cramps in my calves and hands. I have no way of relaxing my muscles as I ascend. With the top in sight, my muscles quake. Relief. I can make it. I'm already farther than other Stains got. I'm almost there.

I reach up to find the next ledge to grab onto.

Nothing.

I kick my foot out, dragging the side of my boot along the cliff's surface.

Again. Nothing.

It's a straight drop to the lake and the red rocks below.

I reach again. Praying that there's something, anything to cling to.

Nothing.

I have to edge back around the side above where I started. I press my body against the sheer rock, pretending it hugs me back. I pretend that something, anything, is holding me.

As I skirt closer to being above solid round, the Canid Carey sniffs and paces, hungry for me. It doesn't help me to think about my predator skulking below. I never want to see those empty sockets again.

That resolve is short-lived when there's a sharp intake of breath and rush of air. I scream when the Canid launches at me. I'm just barely out of its reach. The flat plane is only a few feet above me.

I scramble up The Mount's face, clumps of red stone crumbling under my feet. I gulp breaths as the red rock falls through the air and hits the Canid on the muzzle. Its jaws snap and he shakes the crumbles from its fur. It jumps again. Its hot breath leaves its mouth as a growl, frustrated by all this trouble over an easy prey. I climb higher, trying to block out the jumping and scraping, again and again.

The beast takes a moment, growling below me. When my hand reaches up and lands on the plateau, I let out a sob. Tears stream down my face. I'm able to lift my upper body and stretch both arms out on the flat ground. There's a large divot in the center. It's like a shallow basin. That's where I'm supposed to put Donny's ashes. The pull pulses through me, alive with my revelation, glowing within because I'm sure of what my purpose is. It's so clear. Donny's essence needs to be emptied into that hollow, and it will make him whole again. It will set him free.

I lurch backward. The tearing sends shockwaves through me. The Canid clamps down on my backpack. I scramble and dig my fingers, elbows, anything into the ground. There's a loud rip and snap as it tears off one of the pockets. The backward jerks that almost sent me falling into its jaws finally cease. It lets out yips like excited laughter. I scramble and kick to get myself completely onto the plateau.

My limbs melt with exhaustion. I can't get my legs back under me. My arms don't push up from the ground to help me stand. I manage to crawl over to the hollow's rim while the Canid pounds the ground and scratches at the side of The Mount.

The hollow is the size and shape of a small, shallow tub. I tear at my backpack. My hands shake so badly that I can barely sit the pack down. My cramped hands struggle to grip the zipper. The pull is practically singing in my ears and makes my skin buzz. I'm only able to partially open the pack before those huge claws sink their way into The Mount's face, followed by the sneering, frothing Canid Carey.

Its shoulders are high while its head hangs low, snaking its way toward me. Its nothingness eyes fixed. I stumble to my feet. It launches itself through the air. I roll to the side and the beast lands inches from my head. I stand up and run on wobbly legs across the plateau.

It's futile. The Canid keeps pace alongside me, pushing me to turn and run to my left. With the edge nearing, I have a fleeting thought of just flinging myself off the side and onto the red rocks below. It's better to break my neck than be devoured by the Canid. It's better to break my neck than be consumed. It's better to break my neck than be satisfaction for a demon.

As I run right up to the edge, there's a screech. It's Skeletor, diving straight for The Canid's face. Skeletor claws and flaps at the Canid Carey's death eyes. It howls and rears back. It claws at its own face. The elongated chest rises and falls, huffing at the vulture. Skeletor claws and fights while all I do is stand there, frozen, clutching my half-opened backpack.

The Canid finally makes contact with Skeletor, sending him sprawling across the plateau. He lands in a heap. His wings snap at irregular angles, just a pile of red-caked feathers. A sob escapes my lips and tears run down my raw, wind-torn cheeks. The Canid tries to train its mangled gaze on me. Dark, textured blood oozes into its eye sockets. The Canid then lays its ears back flat, revealing all its rotten teeth as it growls.

Sightlessly, it lunges right at me.

I try to sidestep, but his jaws clamp and tear at my backpack. It has my pack in its grip, my brother in its jaws. I could have held on. I should have. Without my brother, all of this is pointless. Without my brother, everyone's sacrifices are for nothing.

But I let go. I let go of my brother while he's in the mouth of the Canid Carey, as it catapults itself over the edge of the cliff, free falling.

The beast tumbles and the urn clangs as the Canid and my brother hit a ledge on their descent. The jaws release my brother on impact, and Donny's ashes fly and flutter. He's just a gray cloud that flits in the wind. The Canid's howl of despair is interrupted with the snap and pop of breaking bones as its body hits far below.

The Canid Carey is gone.

And so is everyone else.

# CHAPTER TWENTY-NINE

I FALL TO my knees while unable to stop myself from staring at the Canid's lifeless body. My brother is nothing. His urn is bent and mangled somewhere along the lapping lake. His ashes are sprawled and sprinkled throughout Hollow Forest, forever to be left in this wicked place. Would he be a Stain now, too? And for what? For Skeletor to be dead? For Laken to be ripped apart? For Wyatt to come back from one nightmare to wake up in another? This is the only home he provided for himself, and I single-handedly destroyed it.

I drag my eyes from staring at the Canid's sprawled carcass. It's difficult to avoid searching for the bits of my brother that sway and twirl through the air, away from me.

My arms are empty. I'm not clutching, grasping, reaching, or carrying anything. My limbs just hang at my sides as I trudge to Skeletor's heap. No breath enters or leaves his body. I crouch down and let my fingers gently glide through his brilliant red feathers. They are so soft and blow around in the wind that sweeps across the top of The Mount.

"Thank you," I say, tears dripping into his plumage and some of the ruddy clay rubs away to reveal his original white underneath. "I'll never forget what you did, you brave, brave bird."

The pull is still strong, drawing me to the shallow depression in the middle of the plateau. I fall to my knees and crawl into the indentation. I curl up on my side. There's nothing but my singing skin and insurmountable grief.

I weep for Laken who is probably bleeding and sinking to the bottom of the surrounding waters.

I weep for Skeletor, who once was majestic and blotted out the sun with his wingspan, only to be reduced to a crumpled heap of feathers.

I weep for Wyatt, who is no more than an apparition, and turns to mist when all he wants is to be solid.

I weep for my brother. My brother, who taught me how to ride a bike. My brother who could always make me laugh. My brother who held me close and was my one source of family when everything felt like it shifted. And was taken from me, by my parents, by pills, by a boy, by death, by demons.

I think of my brother's curls and twinkling black eyes, always scheming. The time he taught me how to put on eyeliner. When he took me to the hospital after Jacob. When we snuck out to go to an underground EDM concert. When I woke up in the middle of the night from him snoring on the air mattress in my dorm. When he told me he was gay, before anyone else. The way he used to ruffle my hair on my head, always messing it up at the worst times. When we staggered, drunk on the beach, and sat for hours talking next to the waves and under the stars. Donny, my big brother. I almost hear his voice now.

"Angelita. Don't cry."

But how can I stop? The dam is open. I'm swimming in sadness. It's a never-ending grief. It's death by memories.

"Angela. I'm right here."

There's a soft nudge on my shoulder and I turn my head, squinting. Donny is kneeling next to my curled body, shining so brightly that I can't open my eyes all the way. I sit up. My head pounds and my cheeks stream with tears. I have to shield my eyes from how bright Donny is.

"It's you," I say. I shut my eyes and reach for him.

I grasp him and he holds me back. He's strong, alive, and comforting. He warms me from the inside out. I don't want to let go. I'm lighter than air. The whole world fades as I center myself on what's right in front of me. My brother. My big brother.

"It's me," he says. "And you're okay. You're so brave, Angelita. You never should have risked—"

I cut him off. "I knew what I needed to do. I knew you wouldn't be safe without me."

A sob escapes him and shudders under my embrace. He clasps the back of my neck to keep me close.

"I've missed you so much," I say.

"I know," he says. "Without you, I would've been stuck forever. You've set me free. You've made me remembered, and that's what matters."

My mind races to what Jessica told me. She said to take his *essence* to where the pull took me. I thought that meant his ashes, but it's so much more.

I lean back, trying to look at Donny, in all of his radiance. My memories of him recorded who he was as a person, and will continue to keep him alive.

As if reading my mind, he gently holds my chin. I'm light, almost dizzy.

"That's right. I'll live on forever. Not just in the afterworld, but because of you. Your remembrance is everything. Gracias, Angelita."

His voice is far away. He's brighter now, beaming. His touch on my face wavers and I can't tell if he's real anymore. I have to turn away from his light. My arms and legs wisp into mist. I break apart, just a conglomerate of droplets, shining and radiating in my brother's light. I reach out to hug him again, to just hold him a little longer. But I'm no longer solid. I'm all of my cells broken up, yet still me. I rise and fall in the winds. Everything passes through me, the swirling breezes, the cool waters, the tickling leaves, the dense stones and scratchy bark, until I recollect.

The little bits of me attract to each other, like each droplet in my own vapor has their own pull, connecting them back together. I still reach and reach for my brother, but when my entirety collects, I grasp at nothing and fall to the forest floor.

Twigs and leaves scratch at my stomach and cling to my hair. Dirt sticks to my chin where I fall flat. I sit back on my bare knees, disoriented and with the familiar grieving ache in my heart. My brother is gone for good, and yet he's okay. I know it. But that doesn't make me miss him any less. I wipe at the tears on my face and the dirt and grime on my hands smear across cheeks.

I'm naked and stunned on my haunches. To gain my bearings, I try to steady my wavering gaze. It shifts in and out of focus, the edges of my view blur. I face a sight, one that's familiar but yet from long ago. In front of me is the gate. It has that chain, a laughable barrier for the Fiends that lurk inside.

**KEEP SHUT**, it reads.

I check behind me, not worrying about covering myself. Donny's Jeep sits right where I left it, unassuming and reminding me of the modern world I left behind for so long.

I remain kneeling before the lone gate. Should I walk back in? I have a life there. I have Wyatt. I can rebuild it with him. Wyatt's right. What do I have waiting for me at home? Do I even *have* a home? We could make a new camp. Start over. Build safety with each other.

But I have a job now. I need to keep all the loving memories of Donny alive, to take thoughts of Wyatt into my world, to mourn the loss of the beautiful Laken and striking Skeletor. And one thing I learned for sure was that you can't let the fear of living keep you from doing so.

I stand up on shaking legs, trying to center myself on limbs that are mine again. When I finally breathe and move on my own, I walk down the little hill where I parked Donny's Jeep. I don't look back.

# CHAPTER THIRTY

THE REAL WORLD is more fast-paced than I remember it. When I get back to my apartment, it doesn't have that heaviness it had before. It's a normal place. No eyes on me, nothing scurrying within the walls.

I let my phone charge. It's foreign in my hands while I tidy my place that looks like it's been ransacked. There's a note on my tiny kitchen table from my parents. It's written in worried, scrawled script and expresses their concern about my where-abouts. They beg me to contact them. I turn on my phone. The date is unbelievable.

I was in the forest for a little over a month, but my phone says that it's been four days. That can't be. After several calls to my frantic parents, my work, and the police department that had a missing person's report out on me, I try to clear everyone's worst fears.

My family isn't having it. They berate me for not updating them. They cry over the phone about how I scared them. They sucker me into going out to dinner with them so we can "talk." I pick Donny's and my favorite place on the boardwalk, and we meet there.

My parents are quiet while we eat sea salt and vinegar fries. The seagulls call their sad cry while we munch, shoulder to shoulder, facing the ocean.

"I did it for Donny, you know." I break the silence.

"Did what?" My dad asks.

"I went away. I did it to remember him." My voice shakes. "And you need to remember him, too."

"Of course we remember him," my mom blurts. Her voice, usually soft, is breathy, desperate, and angry. "We will never forget our child. He was my little—" her voice catches. "Mijo," she whispers.

My dad wraps an arm around each of us.

"Is that what this nonsense is about? You running away like that's what you thought? That everyone just forgot about Donny? Our sweet boy?"

"Well, you kicked him out. You only have bad memories, and that affects things," I say. My throat is scratchy. I want to scream at them, slap them. But I'm tired. I'm so tired.

"We didn't agree with him," my dad says. "But we never stopped loving him." Tears roll down his face.

He looks so much like Donny, sometimes. Donny always had his strong, defiant jaw and thick hair. His sad eyes. I guess I have those, too.

"We didn't understand him," my mom said, "but we will always hold him close to our hearts."

I don't know if she was referring to his sexuality or addiction, but I know that's the most endearing my parents have been toward my brother.

"Just promise me you'll think of him," I say.

"Siempre." My mom squeezes my hand.

They give me tearful hugs before they go. I stare at the waves for a long time after they leave. I don't realize I'm walking until I'm bathed in the familiar neon light. Gaspara's Sight, it reads. Jessica and Gaspara wait at the door as if they expect my company.

Before I say anything, Jessica wraps me in a tight hug. "I saw you. I would get glimpses of you. I tried to project messages. I tried to reach out. And I saw what you did. I'm so so sorry, Angela. I had no idea."

She pulls back and stares at me. There are dark circles under her bloodshot eyes. Her hair is frazzled instead of silky straight like the first time I met her. Gaspara gently rests her gnarled hand on my shoulder.

"Jessica has learned that visions don't provide the whole truth, and how to proceed with caution. But really, we are both glad you are okay. Please, have some tea," she says.

We take a seat and sip tea. The words pour from my mouth as I hold the warm mug. I tell them everything I experienced in Hollow Forest. I tell them about the Canid Carey, about Laken and Skeletor, about the lake, the wildflower meadow, about sweet, loving Wyatt. Of how I was able to embrace Donny one more time. They nod at the parts they must have seen while gasping in disbelief in other moments.

"Your stories and fond memories of your brother are what keep him in a good place. It's what holds him, uplifts him. And the only reason he is there today is because of your love and bravery. He is lucky to have someone who cares for him this much. It's so rare to find such a strength."

I immediately picture Wyatt. Of how he died for me. Of how he's cursed to return time and again to Hollow Forest.

Gaspara takes my empty mug and peers inside at the leftover tea leaves. "You still have so much love to give." Her smile is sad.

Jessica peers into the cup as well, her brows furrowed. "Your heart – it breaks for Wyatt, yes?"

"Yes." My eyes prickle with tears.

"Listen to your heart," Gaspara says. "It will always give you the right answers. Maybe not easy, and maybe not as clearly as you'd like, but it will tell you."

Jessica rolls her eyes. "My Nonnina is trying to say that it doesn't have to be over with Wyatt. That you can still find him."

"Absolutely not! Have you learned nothing, Jessica? Her heart will tell her the rest. You are too specific. She could interpret that as going back to Hollow Forest. Words have such power, and you throw them around like they're nothing."

"I'm sorry, Nonnina." Jessica's tired eyes are gloomy with her embarrassment.

"Never mind, child. Angela, don't listen to our words. They're just reaffirming what you already feel. Deep inside, you know how to end the aching in your heart."

*

I sleep too much. I do my calls for work and then I just lay in bed, watch television, and stare at the ceiling. At first I brush it off as recovering from my time away, a twisted form of jet lag. But really, it's an escape. I don't have to hurt so much when my eyes are closed. Missing Donny is a dull ache with reassurances that he's alright. But Wyatt? He's a sharp stab in my ribs. Someone whose memories brings pain and a relentless replay of all our moments together. Me puking in front of him. Him making the feathered hide for me. Me killing the horned Jackalope. Him teaching me how to fish. Me almost killing him with a knife. Him kissing me. Us making love. Me punching him in the nose. Him soaring and fighting. Him disappearing. Just fading away.

That's what I find myself re-watching in my mind the most. His body parts disappear, dismembered. Just his mouth telling me to go. He puffs into vapor, slow and steady like an hourglass. It's too much. So I drown it out. With T.V. Land and long sleeps.

I wake up from one of my sleeping stints to gunshots. They come from a PPK that the one and only 007 agent, this time played by George Lazenby, holds at his hip.

It cuts to a commercial break that advertises the all-night James Bond marathon, starting with Sean Connery and jumping to Daniel Craig and Lashana Lynch.

"The name's Bond. James Bond," George Lazenby says, before a cutaway to him holding a blonde with big hair in his arms.

Wyatt loved Bond so much. I can't believe the first thing we talked about was 007. Even the way he introduced himself. Wyatt. Just Wyatt. Ridiculous. We went through so much and he hadn't even given me his full name. I fight anger back when that part of our encounter together replays and replays. Wyatt. Just Wyatt.

And it hits me. I've been so blind.

# CHAPTER THIRTY-ONE

WEST VIRGINIA REALLY is wild and wonderful. The mountains rise and fall while clouds tumble overhead, leaving shadows that sweep across the land. It reminds me of Skeletor's giant shadow when his wide wingspan cast sweeping silhouettes. I swallow and try to dislodge the lump that forms in my throat. I find the turn and Donny's Jeep rumbles onward.

*Wisteria Manor*

The name of the building is scrawled in beautiful script and stamped into a copper sign. There's a mixture of nervousness and relief as I find a parking space. I open the heavy door and approach the woman at the entry desk. She has on thick, wire-rimmed glasses connected to a gold chain. She peeps over the top of her frames to make eye contact.

"Can I help you?"

"Um, yes. I called yesterday and spoke to a Mrs. Batiste? It was about," I clear my throat, "visiting my, um, cousin."

"Oh yes! That's me!" Her voice then drops low so that I have to lean in close. "I know you're a good friend, but you get the 'only family' thing. So I had to jot you down as his cousin. But it's been so long since, well, I'm just glad that he's going to have a visitor."

I nod as she scurries around the entry room and out to greet me. She immediately walks past me and leads the way. I need a quick pace to keep up. She can't be more than five feet, but by her sure steps, someone would think she's a tall man. I watch her long, gray hair pulled in tight braids sway like a metronome as she leads me to the common area. We pass by several rooms where nurses are helping people take their medicine.

"He was more lucid about a week ago. I don't know if you'll be able to get much out of him now. But honey, I've been a nurse for the better part of 30 years, and visiting patients helps. It really does. I tried to tell his family – well, you know him. You probably already know his story. I'm just grateful you're here. He's over there. I'll leave you to it."

"Thank you," I say, scanning the room.

Mrs. Batiste pats my arm and walks away with her quick gate. My eyes dart, frantically searching. I jump from rocking chairs, to people playing cards, to someone mumbling to themselves. I almost miss him in the back corner, sitting still.

It's Wyatt alright, but not the vibrant, strong, and confident man I know. This person is more of a husk. His limbs are small and thin as if they've atrophied. I make my way across the room, forcing myself to walk slowly. His eyes remain distant. They flick and stare at nothing, following things that aren't in our world.

"Wyatt?" I say.

No response. No eye contact. No movement or acknowledgment.

I pull up a chair to sit close to him. His head is shaved. His beautiful dreads, nonexistent. His eyes are sunken in and blackened underneath like he hasn't slept in months. He has a sickly pallor. He's ashen instead of his deep, healthy skin tone. His cracked lips move, but no sound comes out. He's dreaming with his eyes open. I hold his hand. So cold. Goosebumps dot his skin. He always said how cold he is here. How it's lonely, white, bright, and freezing.

"Can I—can I get a blanket?" I asked a nurse who walks by.

"Who for?" he asks.

I point to Wyatt.

"Yep. He can have one. I'll be back."

"Thank you," I whisper.

I rub Wyatt's arms in the meantime in an attempt to warm him. He has a bracelet on. It reads:

Wyatt, Justin "Just". AA Male.

DOB: 08/18/1989

PCP: Dr. Lightfoot

Allergies: Sulfa

I shake my head as tears form but I keep rubbing his arms. My fingers brush against raised bumps and scratches that had long since healed along his skin. I stop to inspect them. There are long cuts that are now keloidal scars. They're raised, shiny and prominent. Has he been hurting himself? The cuts, bashes, and bites are everywhere. Even his nose looks broken and reset.

I stand up to investigate further. I hover over him and his unseeing eyes. And there it is. Where his neck meets his shoulder is a scar right where I stabbed him with Totto. These are all the times he's died. Marks and tattoos of his survival. I'm misty as my fingers graze the upraised, glossy scar.

"Here you are." The nurse is back, handing me a white blanket. I try to wipe away my tears, but my vulnerability just makes my crying worsen as I take the blanket.

"Hey," The nurse says. "You alright?"

I shake my head. "This isn't the Wyatt I know."

I can't take in his forlorn body right now. It's too much.

His eyebrows are creased with concern and sadness. "He's still in there, you know. It's never easy for family and caregivers after such a terrible car accident, especially when their loved ones are in a catatonic state. But by being supportive like you are now, and getting him specialized care in this private facility, it can really help. I know how hard it can be, though, to see them like this. Especially when you've known them before. But Just has his good days, too."

I nod, clutching the blanket to my chest.

"Hang in there," he says and leaves me alone again.

I drape the blanket over him and sink down in the chair next to him. I smooth it out and tuck the ends around the sides of his lap so he's snug.

I take a deep breath and scoot my chair so I sit directly facing him. I lean in close and reach out to gently trace the crooked bridge of his nose. Is that from when I punched him? Or is it from another time?

I yelp when he reaches out and grasps my wrist. His grip is strong but doesn't hurt. I could yank my hand away, but I don't. I want his touch. He blinks and he's here.

"Wyatt?"

His chapped lips part. With a shaky voice he says, "An-A-Angela."

"Yes," I say a little too loudly. "Wyatt, I'm here."

The corners of his mouth creep up and his eyes widen, just a little bit. It's a small move, but significant. I see him and he sees me.

I lean in close. "Just? Your fucking name is Just Wyatt? You shit." But I can't help but smile through my tears.

His lips quiver, struggling to make words. "I t-told y-y-y-you my n-n-name."

"Well, you told me in like a riddle or some shit. If I hadn't been watching a 007 movie, I would have completely missed it." I give his arm a little swat, which makes him smile. Truly smile.

"The C-Canid is g-goo-good camo."

"Good! You deserve to use its skull. I hope you get payback from the hide."

His smile broadens, looking sly.

"I miss you," I say.

"I l-love you," he says.

I cry even more.

I hug him. It's awkward and his arms quake and jerk at odd angles to wrap around me. But I don't care. It's the best hug I've ever had. His arms can't cling to me long, and they drop to his lap. I pull back and his eyes still see me, but his jaw is a little bit open and off-set.

"Wyatt?"

He doesn't say anything, but he still focuses on me.

"Wyatt, we did it. We got Donny to the top. My brother is going to be okay."

"G-goo-g." He huffs but he can't form his words.

"I saw him and everything. I'm so sorry. You had to sacrifice so much. Did Laken," I choke and have to clear my throat. "Did Laken make it?"

His eyes crinkle at the corners. I flood with relief when I realize he's smiling.

"Thank God. Are you alright? Did you find a new camp?"

But he's gone. He clouds over again and is vacant once more. He's back at the Hollow.

"I'm so, so sorry, Wyatt." I put both of his lax hands in mine. "You need to be here. *I* need you here. I think," I clear my throat. "I think that everyone has their own gate they need to keep shut.

Mine was in person. Like, I physically saw it. But yours is in your mind." One of his hands twitches and I clutch them tighter. "We need to find a way to keep that gate shut. Keep the Fiends out. But until then, I'm not leaving you. I'm here, always, no matter what. I won't abandon you like how you didn't abandon me." His eyes dart, following a phantom. "I love you, Wyatt."

And we sit together, in silence, with him in his world, and me in mine.

We would find a way to close the gate. We would find a way to Keep Shut.

We would reunite.

We had to.

# AFTERWORD

Although this book only captures one person's experience with grief, conditional love, and trauma, I hope that other survivors can discover that they are not alone. We are all trying to navigate our personal forests and Fiends. I hope those who are battling their own Hollow know that they are seen, they are valid, and they have the natural intuition and supports that will guide them through it.

# ACKNOWLEDGMENTS

Thank you to the fighters out there. You inspire me and fellow survivors to keep our heads up.

Thanks to my husband, who is always supportive and ready for me to throw a crazy story idea his way.

To my beta readers, your involvement is invaluable. Thanks for your encouragement.

To all the close friends and family members who gave me insight and support.

To my editor, Stephanie Cohen, thank you for your knowledge-able and detailed feedback. *Ashes* wouldn't be what it is today without your expertise.

Triple C Shops created a fabulous logo for Twin Trees Press and the author portrait editing. Thank you for your keen eye and creativity.

Dale Robbins, you are a fabulous author, an outspoken person, and a true inspiration in the writing community. I'm so happy to have met you and thankful for such a stellar person to be my best friend.

Thanks to Bolt From Blue studios for the conceptual design of the blood-fed Ruminant and giving invaluable feedback.

*Thank You*

*Thank you for reading Ashes.*

*Feel free to leave a review on Amazon and Goodreads.*

*If you'd like to be updated on future endeavors, please sign up for my mailing list. Visit https://ionawayland.wixsite.com/author*

# ABOUT THE AUTHOR

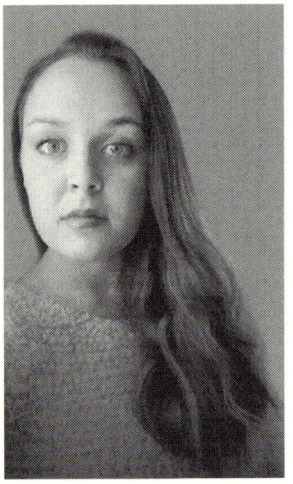

Iona Wayland is a Writer, book lover, and tea enthusiast. She considers herself a child of the forest, and is a devoted animal mom and mental health advocate. She depicts aspects of the human experience often in fantastical ways. Common themes of her work include: grief, surviving trauma, and finding purpose and strength.

Made in United States
Orlando, FL
11 October 2022